MW01714134

The Guardian Angel Level

CHUCK MICHAEL OSTAN

Strategic Book Group

Disclaimer: Language/Situations

The Guardian Angel Level is a Christian book. I being a Christian wrote it to relate the message that is learned during the spiritual, mental, and emotional evolution working in frontline nonprofit and social work.

Unfortunately, to relate these experiences accurately, it had to be told realistically. There are graphic situations, violence, and strong language. This aspect could not be diminished and expect that the reader would get the full impact of the actual experience. For this reason, some Christians and non-Christians alike may object to the subject matter. It is the spiritual message behind it, however, that it is hoped that people will understand. I hope that this book gives the reader both edification and understanding.

Strategic Book Group
P. O. Box 333
Durham, CT 06422
www.StrategicBookClub.com

ISBN: 978-1-61204-127-8

Book Design: Judy Maenle

Dedication

This is a dual dedication, first to the Lord Jesus Christ, my Savior. Second, though, I dedicate this book to my wife, Barb. She is truly the finest person I have ever personally known. Her love is golden, her faith is true, her direction is straight, and her loyalty is to the death. Further, to me she is a kind of hero, in a spiritual sense. She doesn't have hidden agendas like so many others I have known. For this reason, I hope that this book is a success, for her more than for me. While I have been a Guardian Angel for others, she has always been my Guardian Angel.

HEBREWS 12:6-11—*For whom The Lord loves he chastens, and scourges every son whom he receives.*

EPHESIANS 6:12—*For we wrestle not against flesh and blood, but against principalities, against powers, against the rulers of the darkness of this world, against spiritual wickedness in high places.*

ROMANS 8:38, 39—*For I am persuaded that neither death, nor life, nor angels, nor principalities, nor things present nor things to come, Nor height, nor depth nor any other creature, shall be able to separate us from the love of God, which is in Christ Jesus our Lord.*

Contents

PART III: Superstar Social Worker Syndrome

PART IV: The Guardian Angel Level

Preface

Before we address the life-changing experiences that affect those in the helping professions, some groundwork should be laid pertaining to the creation and operation of nonprofit and social work agencies. Social work/nonprofit, the medical profession, fire fighting, and even police work could be considered helping professions. My experience has been exclusively with nonprofit and social work, though I do believe that some of my observations could be considered pertinent across the board.

For the purposes of this book, however, these observations are specific to nonprofit and social work. By the same token, though national and international statistics are similar, I can only comment on the experiences in the region where I lived. It should be said at this juncture that the information and experiences in this book are a fictionalized account based on my observations. The first statistical reality we will deal with is the fact that a frontline worker in nonprofit or social work agencies (in Canada) lasts an average of five years. Burnout, meltdown, resignation, termination, and attrition (and rarely, promotion) are some of the reasons these workers are so vulnerable.

This is a brutally enlightening statistic considering that it takes some education to become a caseworker or even a residential worker in these agencies. A BSW (Bachelor of Social Work), an SSW (college diploma equivalent) or at least an addiction workers certificate and applicable experience is required. So why do so many young people and even older reformed addicts and workers from other sectors of the working population choose this field as a way to make a living?

It is the allure of the possibility of helping individuals. To help troubled people, such as addicts, those with mental health issues or disabilities, or the homeless population in general, either on a personal level or en masse, is a chance to make a difference by helping mankind. In other words, this is the idealistic objective and an admirable idealism in these days and times. The reality is, however, that it is not that simple. The universities and colleges that offer these courses do not prepare their students for the reality of being a frontline worker. The skills of helping that include empathetic listening, inclusive responding and paraphrasing, and effective case planning are seldom successful. In fact, success occurs in only about eight percent of cases.

The people who mostly change are the workers not the clients. As a worker, you will see addiction, disease, deceit, disability, mental health issues, and death. You will see far too much in a compressed time period and it will change your perspective not only on frontline work but also on life in general. It is a system that is mired in red tape and social injustice. The population of the addicted and homeless is almost beyond help. They are typically older, chronically alcoholic or drug dependant, unemployed, mentally ill, or physically ill, and the assistance they are offered for their problems is primarily a Band-Aid solution that is not a conclusive solution or cure.

In this population of homeless, there is also a percentage of street youth and a criminal element. These include former prison inmates, those on probation and the scammers and conmen that survive on the street by illegal means. Some of these take advantage of the system by scamming government checks, selling their own prescriptions as well as illicit drugs, and taking advantage of those in poverty, those with mental health issues, and the elderly.

This quarter or third of the homeless population has no intention of bettering themselves or leaving the system; in fact, exploiting the system is their living. They work under the table paying no taxes, abusing services like shelters, drug cards, and bus passes while hiding their money in different ways, such as through a friend or family member's bank accounts. They are also the most demanding and militant when things don't go their way. However, the entire disenfranchised homeless population does not comprehend the difference between a frontline worker and those who make the policies. To many clients, they all represent the establishment and therefore, the enemy. When a client does not receive his welfare check on time—or a drug card or a bus pass—it is the frontline worker who takes the brunt of the abuse, which can include threats, anger and even attacks.

Meanwhile, the administration person or policy maker up in the office has no real understanding of what the frontline worker does or deals with. These clients are usually given a slap on the wrist by administrators and authorities and allowed back into the shelter when they misbehave. From a management perspective, the fact is that the bottom line must be maintained. The beds must stay full so that funding can continue and that is top priority for the administrator.

It is still about money, like any other business. We will get into the logistics of what that all really means later. Besides these issues, most homeless shelters and program staff are swamped with clients and are severely understaffed and underpaid. The work is emotionally draining and the successes are few. There are many casualties among this population and the frontline worker sees them all.

Some tolerate these disappointments and hurts better than others. The failure or death of clients is always hard when a relationship has been formed. In the long run, only a few workers last to do this kind of work and of those, many become jaded or bitter. It is a statement on the condition and circumstances that have led to the burnout and meltdown of many within these professions. In the city that the statistics from this book are based on, of the little over 400,000 population, 100,000 people were living on the poverty line. This is a huge drain on the system.

So in this system that consists of so many agencies set up to help (the homeless, addicted and those with mental health issues and physical disabilities), why is there so much poverty, tragedy, and death? Let's start with the government programs and policies that fund this money and the various agencies that this money is contracted to.

Let us then look at the application of these funds for use among the client population and how the client population typically uses these funds. Funding is provided by the government in response to a proposal from an agency for homeless, addictions, disability, mental health, or cognitive skills services.

These agencies that constitute the core of providers have usually been in business for years. These agencies have made their proposals and received funding years ago and now simply renew their contract yearly or are automatically funded. These core services start with homeless shelters and offer everything from medical care and prescriptions to counseling and income support or trusteeship. These government-sanctioned funds provide $40 per bed per night (at the time of the writing of this book) for an occupied shelter bed. Extra funding is provided for counseling, medical, and statistical services. As well as these, there are always new programs that are being created as offshoot programs of these existing core services. Special disability sections of the shelters, which pay doctors, nurse practitioners, nurses and health care aids, are funded separately and are well provided. Nurse practitioners can earn up to $43 per hour; nurses, up to $38 per hour; personal support workers and caseworkers, $18 per hour; and the frontline residential worker earns only $15 per hour. It is estimated that the biggest shelter in this test city earned $80,000 to $120,000 per month in income before expenses. This includes donations. There are no taxes because all these organizations are either part of a religious denomination or are non-denominational, and as such are eligible for tax-exempt status based on religious exemption. These facts and figures do not take into account the offshoot programs but just the shelters alone. Apart from nurses, doctors, and caseworkers, administrators such as executive directors, directors, assistants, managers, and supervisors are also paid extremely well.

Introduction

Some of the hierarchy in the administration of these nonprofit and social work agencies act like the CEOs of major corporations and drive around in high-end vehicles with personalized license plates like "Charity Bob" or "Pas. (Pastor) Anne." Meanwhile, the frontline worker lives to work and works to live, under-staffed, over-worked, and not well paid. The clients also (those who do try) work for temp agencies, the income from which doesn't even pay their rent or provide enough money for basic needs like dental care, drugs, or glasses. From the client's perspective, the reason for their lot is partially a system that is a showpiece of perception, but in reality, does not work. One caseworker typically takes care of ninety to one hundred clients. Further, the programs that are created for this population are quick fixes that don't solve the problem over the long term. Shelters, for example, are supposed to not only provide shelter for homeless clients but are to try to re-indoctrinate these clients back into society. This rarely happens. The shelter system has become a revolving door (much like the penal system) for clients who have stopped trying and have become increasingly disenfranchised and rebellious in the bargain.

The business of homelessness and addictions has evolved in a displaced society to the point that these services have become among the biggest employers in some regions. In what we will call "Test City," social work and the helping professions were the number two employers in the region after health services. In business terms, this means that the number two employer in the region does not create a product or bring anything tangible to the region but is a deficit employer running a business on the backs of taxpayers and government. The recycling, placement, and/or eventual disposal of these human beings have become big business and the new twenty-first century condition. More prominent communities have also jumped on the bandwagon, mostly not realizing the truth about the homeless situation.

Golf tournaments for charity, charity drives, furniture, food and cash donations are all part of the community's way of contributing to help the homeless situation. Doing your part to help is one thing, however, but not having the stigma of homelessness in your prominent community is another. When a homeless person should appear in one of these prominent bedroom communities, they are usually whisked away to the city center, which provides all the services. From this point on, we will call this city "Test City" to not implicate the real city and because this city basically became an experiment and homeless dumping ground.

A homeless person in Test City could get three meals a day, a voucher for a full set of clothing including work boots, bus fare, medical services, and a street allowance. In this community, there were four shelters, each of which could accommodate a client for fifteen days consecutively. A person would never be without shelter within a one-month period. If a person had a reason for an extension he could stay in a shelter up to forty-two days. It would then be required at this point that they only stay out for ten days before returning to the same shelter. There is not a lot of initiative to try, especially if failure has been the blueprint of your life. Besides mental health issues, lack of training, and illness, the main contributing factor to homelessness either before or after is addictions. Although every agency at least has a resident addictions worker or a referral contact for clients to treatment or pre-addictions services or aftercare, these facilities are expensive and hard to get full funding for. Dealing with these kinds of clients and issues are messy and most homeless agencies choose not to get directly involved in addiction services because of this.

Death, overdoses, staff defections, trafficking and the criminal element are within the shelters and particularly in addictions services. Before ID was required (and some shelters still don't require it), people could stay at shelters under false names, which was going underground. Addictions are the basis of the homeless problem, however. It is an epidemic among the clients and even sometimes workers. The nature of addictions is that everyone is somewhat addicted to something. It could be coffee, chocolate, and foods of all types, gambling, sexual addictions, shopaholic, kleptomania, drugs, or alcohol. It could also be attitude addictions, like pride (to the point where you can't admit you are wrong about anything), selfishness (to the point where you can't share anything), or cleanliness (to the point that everything must be sanitized).

Some of these behaviors cross the line from being addictions to becoming full-blown mania or psychosis. The point is that everyone has some behavior they cannot control. The objective is to beat the more destructive behaviors and trade them for more mundane ones so that you can operate somewhat normally. That is easier said than done for an addicted personality, however. These personalities must fill that black hole inside left by childhood neglect, abuse, or disappointment (with something) and these feelings will be all-encompassing until this is accomplished. Workaholic is a popular trade-off and is usually the most inherited of addictions.

The world loves a hard worker, especially big business, but even smaller companies and nonprofits find this addiction in people very useful. The point from an administration perspective is that if you can motivate these type A personalities to dedicate themselves exclusively to your company (nights, weekends, overtime, on-call), you then have a paid slave, loyal confident, delegate, and a second set of eyes. Workaholics love filling their time with these kinds of tasks because it usually leaves little time to deal with what is really important, one's self. Be fiercely loyal but keep busy and above all, never be alone. This lack of self-awareness usually precedes a crash or a huge change—a baptism of fire, if you will.

If you are this chosen employee, don't lose your focus or your perspective in the meantime. Don't have a second addiction like being a closet drinker or drug user. Don't burn out or get ill either, or question the status quo. If you do, you will find your shining star become tarnished very quickly. You will become a casualty relegated to the garbage heap of burned-out soldiers. This does happen as quickly in nonprofits as it does in big business. Because the reality is that nonprofit, social work and charitable organizations are big business and like any other big business, the bottom line is profitability. This statement is fact for many agencies and workers, but not all.

The homeless shelter itself is only the original or base operation of nonprofit or charitable organizations administrated by religious organizations. The offshoot or satellite programs often equal or supersede the original hostel format for success stories and potentially more extensive funding and profitability. Food lines usually require a $10 a month contribution from a client, which would entitle the patron to one meal a day: breakfast, lunch, or dinner. This is a very inexpensive way to eat for the client.

Imagine if you will, though, how much money the shelter might make on a pay food line in an atmosphere like Test City where over 100,000 people were on the poverty line and half of them used some form of food supplement help like food banks or food lines although some food lines are free. The tentacle of the nonprofit and charity world does not end there, however. There are parking concessions for events in the vicinity (employing attendants), street clinics (employing doctors and nurses, funded by the government to keep this extra clientele from hospital emergency rooms), programs that care for those without an address who are released from hospitals. There are also subsidized housing and facilities for battered women, which are a nonprofit industry of their own, not to mention private rooms in the shelters and offsite housing, which is the future of housing for the homeless.

As governments look for ways to get the homeless off government assistance and out of homeless shelters, offsite housing has become the new pinup program for nonprofits. Provide government subsidized apartments for chronically homeless, supported by medical and social work support staff and intervention, and these people will be self-sufficient. This is the theory. In reality, however, this plan has always been and only will ever be partially successful. If the majority of the homeless population could manage and maintain personal living with the cognitive skills required, they would probably have never needed a homeless shelter. Doing laundry, managing bills and finances, cooking and maintaining the cleanliness of their environment and their own personal hygiene are many times beyond the abilities of these clients, even with the token support that is offered. These are the reasons why these clients wind up in the shelter system to begin with and usually wind up back there when independent living fails, even with support. Usually once these programs fill their housing units, the program is considered a success and the support staff is reduced to a skeleton staff. Then the dominos begin to fall exactly as happened with the mental health act decades earlier.

So what has caused a homeless situation that increases by leaps and bounds every year and is in fact an epidemic? The end of industrialization and the dawn of the computer age displaced workers who then wound up on unemployment insurance or welfare roles. Not only this generation was affected but the next generation also and the children of that next generation.

Unemployment and welfare roles have been cut several times since. Whenever the government needs to cut funds, these are the programs that are the most susceptible. In addition to the addiction issues, cognitive skills and environmental displacement, there are the mental health issues.

The mental health act that was passed in 1990 states that a person who is not a danger to themselves or others cannot be held against their will no matter how severe the mental health issue. The premise of this law was that previous laws and procedures for dealing with mental health issues were archaic, cruel, and unjust. The reality is that the new mental health act allowed the government to close down or reduce mental health facilities and services. This gave the public a tax cut and the government a tax grab but left legions of those with mental health issues homeless and walking the streets because subsidized housing and homeless facilities could rarely deal with them. Those with mental health issues, addictions and emotional issues aren't the only tragedies in the homeless environment.

I have known an engineer, a professor and a stockbroker, all who became homeless through illness or misfortune. Some had debilitating illnesses, like strokes or heart attacks, or fell on hard times through unexpected expenses, lost assets or had addictions. Many times, there was no family, lawyer, or power of attorney in place to help these people. There was no one to advocate for them and no system to help them, so they lost their assets. Federal, provincial, and state governments continue to squabble over who is responsible for the homeless and funding continues to be cut. Many different strategies will be needed to help the homeless now, and long-term policies to reduce and prevent homelessness in the future, but mismanagement and misappropriation must be addressed.

So after all this is said and done, what is the shelter system and what has it become? It has become a revolving door, with 30 to 40 percent of these clients returning month after month and year after year with no real resolution to their problems. This is only the tip of the iceberg as to what is wrong with the system. The feeling of helplessness that these circumstances bring to workers and clients can be debilitating and can cause apathy and a jaded outlook. The worker and the client are bled dry emotionally. The emotional distress that these circumstances cause can sometimes reach epidemic proportions. It can cause a feeling of disenfranchisement in clients and staff and cause a feeling of rebelliousness and a climate of anti-social feelings and behavior.

In clients, these feelings can manifest themselves in the form of vandalism, theft or attacks on other clients and staff, even the disabled or elderly, for drug money or simple retribution. Vandalism in the shelters can consist of broken toilets, mirrors, fire extinguishers, tables, chairs, doors, and beds. It doesn't make sense when you think about it. These agencies are providing a service (a charity), feeding, clothing, and caring for these people. They are providing a service that in most cases these clients could probably not provide for themselves. Yet their reaction is contempt. Why? Mostly because they have to live this way and they blame the establishment in all forms, even the frontline worker.

Workers are just as damaged in this environment as clients. Burnout and absenteeism are chronic and workers quit or are dismissed on a regular basis. Absenteeism in these agencies is among the worst of any profession. Sometimes to escape for a while or gain a new prospective on their work, a worker might approach a company EAP, which could mean referral to addiction services, counseling or even psychiatric evaluation. The stigma attached, however, is usually more injurious than the cure. This kind of leave is called "Looney Leave" in the industry, and your career is not likely to recover once you have taken a leave of this type. For all these reasons, there isn't much help for workers in the helping professions except for supportive family, friends and one's own experience, maturity, and faith. And that is the glimmer of hope in this situation, that there are still some workers and administrators who are in it to help, even if it's just a few. That is what the helping professions are supposed to be about: the spiritual/emotional evolution of all parties. From a Christian perspective, when that does happen, however rare, it then somehow all makes sense. The new worker entering the social work/nonprofit world does not want to consider these truths during his education or during his indoctrination into this work. If you are a new worker full of promise and empathy, you will be disillusioned very quickly even though you may not be able to share this information with your peers or administration. You will see the homeless panhandling or maybe receiving a donation or otherwise being treated like a fire hydrant or lamppost. You could see your clients arrested for vagrancy, public mischief, harassment, or a variety of other charges. You will see them stigmatized also and categorized as lazy drunks no matter what the circumstances might be by which these people became homeless. You will see them become statistics in a lineup, at the food banks, the shelters, the medical clinics, or the welfare office. Whenever governments need to cut expenditures, these clients are first on the chopping block. They are a barnacle on the underside of the ship we call society. These people are truly society's scar and except for a minority, they are people who have fallen through the cracks through misfortune, through change, addiction, or illness. Remember the old saying, "There but for the grace of God go I." So then, who are the homeless? The answer is they are people just like us.

PART I: New Worker's Syndrome

Introduction

When Mitch stepped into his new role as residential worker and caseworker at a new agency, there were very few people who had any idea what history lay behind him. Mitch was no stranger to frontline nonprofit and social work. He was weaned on counseling and nonprofits, starting with his factory days when he had become a chief steward for the steelworkers. He had no idea then that he would be doing addictions counseling, financial counseling, marriage counseling, and that he would become an emotional support for so many people. In the local steel plant where he worked, the president and vice president were aged men who were ill and nearing retirement. As acting president and vice president, this gave Mitch plenty of opportunities to not only understand the inner workings of unions but the nature of employee problems and the counseling and advocating required to bring about a solution. Mitch was allowed some training to become a more effective advocate. He took all those courses that no one else wanted to take: Management/Labor Relations, Human Resources courses, Landlord/Tenant laws, Addictions Training, Employment Standards, Health and Safety and Labor Law. As a result of this, when the steel plant (that was his base of operations) closed in the late eighties, Mitch was prepared. Mitch knew that the age of industrialization was waning and nearing its end. It was about adjusting and changing, evolving in a changing system in order to survive.

Being a street youth, on his own at age 14, working illegally before he was 16 after being ejected from home, Mitch learned to survive in a hostile atmosphere and this had taught him to evolve and change, to conform to conditions. It was a survival technique that would serve Mitch well in all that he would do in the future.

He returned to school and started a university course in social work and addictions that might eventually end in a Bachelor in Social Work (BSW). Mitch had to work during his educational upgrade. He landed a part-time position as a counselor and residential worker with corrections in a halfway house/treatment center. While he worked in this agency, he continued his education through block courses and correspondence. He obtained his addiction studies certificate, which was a license to be an addictions counselor and most of the way to a BSW.

When it was obvious that the corrections field was too crowded with well-qualified prospective employees, Mitch began applying for other positions within the field. He did well while he was waiting, receiving an abundance of relief shifts because of the rampant absenteeism, not just in this agency but also all across frontline helping professions.

Before long, Mitch landed a full-time position as a residential worker and counselor in a homeless agency administrated by an order of Catholic monks called the New Apostles Center. All aspects of homelessness were dealt with either directly or indirectly by this agency. It was a low-paying position that required an enormous amount of work and commitment. Because this agency was administrated by the monks (with a nun for a director), the operation of this service was directed by their morality, their work ethic, and their religious orientation, specifically Catholicism.

Though dozens of employees fell by the wayside in his tenure, Mitch survived in this atmosphere for eight and one-half years. As a Christian, he looked at it as part of his evolution and testing. The problem with the position was that the monks expected the level of religious commitment from employees that they had even though all the employees did not subscribe to their perception or beliefs. For example, on a twelve hour night shift, a residential worker (RW) was expected to book in clients, deal with security issues, help with the snack, laundry, rounds, paperwork and then cook a breakfast of two fried eggs, cereal and toast for the entire shelter including permanent residents (approximately fifty). After breakfast was done, RWs were expected to clean up and do dishes before they went home.

Not many residential workers lasted long. Mitch, however, had become a shift supervisor, a dorm coordinator, and eventually a subsidized housing worker. Even in this atmosphere of pious, holier-than-thou judgment, which included judging morality, fidelity, commitment, and integrity, Mitch found a way to survive. The members of the order, of course, broke all these rules and more.

Whatever could be said of Mitch, though, it must be said that he did his job and he was loyal. Mitch was work-oriented and did have good organizational skills and could maintain order. Eventually the hypocrisy and inconsistency were too much to take, but that is another book. When a position at the Jesus Saves Kitchen (local mission) came up and an old friend asked him to consider it, he resigned The New Apostles Center for a new direction.

Mitch's relationship with clients was another aspect that contributed to his survival and longevity in this field. He had been a street person himself in this very city and more specifically in the north end where all the shelters were now located. Because of this, many of the clients knew him and respected him, even though they might not all like him.

The Jesus Saves Kitchen was different in that it had a dream of actually rehabilitating the homeless. Their fiat was to nurture and promote from the ranks of the homeless and addicted and actually make them counselors and residential workers themselves. When it began, before it became corrupted, it was the most brilliant idea for a shelter. It removed the "them and us" philosophy and made the clients feel invested in the process. Just by giving them a chore or making them a floor monitor, it gave them assurance and some dignity. It restored some of their self-esteem. Of course, eventually the powers that be decided that you couldn't have former clients in the helping professions. So instead, they hired twenty-year-olds directly from school rather than those with addictions or natural street experience. That's when things really got bad and stupid. Mitch became a front desk supervisor, then an offsite supervisor and then a hostel manager.

The problem with this organization, like all the others of its kind, was that a religious figurehead ran it—someone who was appointed from within the religious ranks because of their moral convictions and their religious affiliations but usually had no clue about the operation or delivery of the services they offered.

Because of this, it is usually decided eventually when the shelter starts to fail (in these agencies) that the financial factor is of the utmost importance: improve the numbers, in other words, fill the shelter at whatever cost to clients and staff, which would increase revenues and provide more effective statistics for obtaining more funding. For this reason, a new hatchet person is usually brought in with a business philosophy but without social work/nonprofit experience. It was usually a hardhearted manager with an eye for budgeting and cost cutting, which usually meant less staff. Although this philosophy of high finance-meets nonprofit charity may work in theory, it does not work in reality, at least not for social work/nonprofit agencies. The reason is very fundamental. When charity becomes a business, it ceases to be a charity. The one thing is in complete contravention to the other and it can only then be hypocritical, ineffective (somewhat dangerous for clients and staff), and ultimately corrupt. When you are not equally considering empathy, security, structure and funding, homelessness can be a messy business. For example, the criminal street element will invade your shelter if you allow them to, which means drug dealing, violence, overdoses, and even death.

Consequences for these offences must be decisive. A one-day suspension or even a week's suspension is not adequate. Sometimes, these clients must be service restricted or barred from these facilities. Yet one- or two-day suspensions are all that shelter operators or administrators are usually willing to give. Their rationale is that these are poor and unfortunate homeless but the reality is that it means empty beds. They would rather deal with the threat than the financial issue. And after all, it is not they who are dealing with it anyway; it's the frontline staff.

Every agency and system must take responsibility. The problem is that there are mental health issues, addictions, and the criminal element in the shelter system. Without having an eye on the suitability of certain clients for your shelter and the security issues involving these clients, tumultuous things can happen. People with these issues disrupt the dormitories, waking, disturbing, and infringing on and even threatening other clients, which may lead to many of these clients leaving. This also goes for very serious addictions and cognitive skills problems until all of the regular homeless trying to work or rehab are weeded out and the problem cases are all that remain.

In the end, you must refer out or get specialized attention for the problem cases that your shelter is not equipped to deal with until your shelter is half empty. If instead you were initially honest about what clients you could accommodate based on staffing and expertise, the more stable clients would stay in a safer, more stable environment and the staff would be less volatile and at risk based on whom they could service. That is better than subjecting all parties to specialized problems that they were never trained to deal with because the rest of the system is dumping on your organization and your organization is trying to make money at any cost.

Go with the honesty and integrity of nonprofits and charity. The numbers of homeless will go where they can get shelter, safety, and support. The money will follow when the honesty comes first. Do not sacrifice the many for the few. All facets of the system must work for mental health, addictions cognitive skills, the elderly and disabilities. The homeless shelters cannot handle them all.

When Mitch saw that the truth was not the answer in this organization either, he resigned his manager's job and set his sights on the Redemption Shelter Center. This was the first shelter he had worked in with a union. Imagine a nonprofit social work system with a union—finally someone to protect the worker as well as the client. Mitch had always thought that this was needed. He started part time as a weekend residential worker but soon moved to full-time caseworker and was voted in as a union rep, when the position became available. Not long after this, the full-time afternoon RW job became available. Rather than stay case manager, which was a more prestigious and a better paying job, he became an RW. He was on the busiest shift, the main shift. He stayed union rep to be close to the action and to advocate for his staff and clients. This is the atmosphere that Mitch eventually found himself in and along with his wife and some very good friends, he found support and a new perspective on the helping professions and hoped he could help humankind in a more profound and meaningful way.

Chapter One

There are firefighters and paramedics and doctors and nurses and social workers and counselors and pastors and priests and volunteers and many, many more. Of all these individuals in all of these helping professions, there are a few that go beyond, those who would sacrifice themselves in certain danger to extend a hand to a friend or stranger. These few we will call *Guardian Angels*, not because they are guardian angels in the traditional sense but because they have taken upon themselves the task of helping their fellow man at any cost. And God bless them in the hope that they themselves are not lost. Most of these have given themselves to helping within the helping professions. I believe this is a Christian concept because most social work/nonprofit agencies in North America and Europe had their start as Christian charities and are still administrated by Christian denominations or are non-denominational Christian organizations.

Basically the mission statement for all these agencies is that helping others in return helps us, and all that we may give to others is returned to us someday.

This all originates in the biblical statement in Eccl 11:1-6—"Cast your bread upon the waters and it will return to you after many days." I don't believe you must be a Christian to begin being a helper, however it is a spiritual journey and an evolution based in traditional Christianity education and instruction and it will not stand the test of time (in my opinion) without this basic aspect. A not so literal example of this would be a guidance counselor or chaplain or union rep or an EAP person or an HR person or even possibly a manager or director in some cases—one who can listen not just to clients but to co-workers with an empathetic ear, sound advice and reflection and is able to offer mentoring.

Mentoring in life knowledge is about experience and emotional spiritual guidance, without being judgmental. Most of those that find themselves in these positions are people of at least middle age with plenty of life experience and a talent for dealing with people. People naturally gravitate to them. These workers often give of their time, their emotions and many times even cross the lines or boundaries to help someone. Mitch found himself in this position and because social work/nonprofit is mostly made up of women (90 percent of the staff at the Redemption Center were female), this whole dynamic made the business of frontline a lot more complicated, which will become apparent later in the story.

On one of his first night shifts in the shelter, Mitch stumbled upon a client from his Jesus Saves Kitchen days, one Randy Humbart. Well known to Mitch, Randy had been asked to leave the Jesus Saves Kitchen (where he had been staying for six months) for being drunk and disorderly. This had only happened a few days previously and Mitch was used to waking Randy in the morning for work when he was at the Jesus Saves Kitchen. Randy was always on the wake-up list. Randy made good money in construction (when he worked) and stashed his money with family and continued to stay in shelters. He drank what he didn't stash, which was a lot. He smoked some pot, also, and even did cocaine on occasion.

On this particular morning at the center, Mitch roused Randy up for his 5:00 a.m. wake up. News was that Randy had indulged beyond reason the night before and was allowed into the shelter on strict instructions that he was to go right to bed. This was at approximately 1:00 a.m. When Mitch shook Randy, there was initially no movement; he was snoring like a freight train. Finally Mitch said, "Come on, Randy, are you alive or what." After several tries, Randy began to rouse somewhat. When Randy saw Mitch's face in a setting where it didn't belong, his first reaction was to think he was dreaming or hallucinating.

"Where the fuck am I?" he said. "This ain't the kitchen."

"Easy, Randy," Mitch said, "I work here now."

"You scared the fuck out of me. Don't do that shit anymore."

Mitch and Randy started laughing louder and louder until other dormitory residents were beginning to wake up and Mitch left the dorm.

At this point in time, Mitch was working weekend nights and relief shifts as an RW and a caseworker. His partner was an eccentric, balding, French Canadian in his late forties named Marcel. His job was night janitor/security. Whatever else might be said about Marcel, he was a voracious worker. The two women they relieved from the afternoon shift were Susan and Julie. There was a certain evening when Mitch was still working nights with Marcel that an East Indian fellow with a huge language barrier decided to book in. He understood enough to do the paperwork for booking in, getting toiletries for shower, shaving and so on. But by time he got a cleaned up and settled in his dorm, dinner was long over. It was well after 11:00 p.m. curfew and most clients were in bed, when Habib returned to the desk disoriented. The rules had been explained to him at book in but he did not understand them. The TV room was closed and everything was dark. As he approached the front security door for entry, Mitch motioned to him, from inside the bubble.

"Press the button at your knees." Clients who were already booked into the shelter had full access. Only clients entering from outside had to be booked in.

Habib looked more confused than ever as he stared at Mitch through the window of the bubble. Mitch was on the phone dealing with a person who needed information while dealing with a client at the desk who was becoming increasingly impatient because he had to wait for his meds.

Mitch could have released the button from the office but he decided not to, hoping that Habib would learn how to gain access himself. Mitch said, "Press the freaking button."

"I cannot find it," said Habib.

"Push it," Mitch said, "just push it."

With that, Habib pulled the fire alarm. Well, Marcel the janitor heard the yelling and swearing through the double security doors and down in the basement where he was mopping. He ran up the stairs. Mitch was still yelling at Habib. "You stupid bugger. What are you doing? That's a fire alarm—see—it's red and it says fire alarm." Other clients were stirring and yelling. Mitch finally got to the fire alarm and got it shut off. Habib was repentant and Mitch did not have the heart to go further and totally demean him.

"It's okay," Mitch said, "but next time, this is the button (he pointed to the button at his knees), that's pushing, the fire alarm is pulling, okay, and don't talk through the window."

Habib sheepishly said "Okay."

The thing about frontline is that because of the amount of emotional, spiritual, and mental upheaval that is experienced while trying to facilitate change or evolution in their clients, the worker also changes. They begin to live clandestinely through their clients to facilitate this change, especially when they can no longer get straight answers from their clients, for example that they are using or selling drugs, or involved in other criminal activity. They begin emotionally investing too much until sometimes they are in crisis themselves. So when the worker has an upheaval in their life because of this evolution or change, where do they go? Certainly not to the clients, though some have been guilty of this. Do they go to the EAP or HR or the administrative people that most workers don't trust? To the union rep or co-workers who they depend on when they're in trouble? Sometimes. But mostly they are on their own.

On a few nights when Mitch had come in to work, he had noticed that five or six of the male clients were surrounding the front desk area, trying to make time with Susan or Julie or both. As soon as Mitch began the transition from their shift to his shift, he began asking the clients if they had business at the desk. If they did not need meds or towels or toiletries, they were asked to move on. This upset the clients and also Julie and Susan. The party was over when Mitch arrived. He was the cranky old curmudgeon.

Eventually, Julie and Susan realized that the clients were not there to chat or to keep them company but only had one thing on their minds. Eventually, the two of them became somewhat jaded and more skeptical of many of the clients' agendas or of taking the clients' friendliness and interest at face value.

On the afternoon shift, on which Susan was the weekend RW (desk person) and Julie was caseworker, a myriad of dramas, adventures, and disasters could take place. On one particular night, their shift had consisted of a couple of ambulance calls for sick clients and a couple of drunk and disorderly clients, which required police, resulting in incident reports and a lot of extra paperwork, as if there wasn't enough paperwork already.

When a drunk and disorderly client shows up and you can't allow them into the shelter because of liability issues, the client usually vents on you. Clients called female staff cunts, bitches and whores and male staff everything else under the sun including queer and goof. When Mitch arrived that night, things had quieted down for the moment but Susan was stressed and emotionally beaten to the core. She started crying as soon as she saw Mitch. Julie had just shown up to the desk when Mitch took Susan back into the meds room so that the clients wouldn't see her cry or hear what she had to say. "Mitch, it was a terrible night; none of the paperwork is done but I have to get out of this fucking place."

"Don't worry, Susan. I'll help you. It's going to be OK. You stay back here and get yourself together. I will watch the desk."

"Thanks, Mitch, thanks so much," said Susan.

When Mitch came out, Julie was at the desk, and as soon as she saw the concern on Mitch's face, she said, "What's wrong?"

"Susan is upset and crying in the back. Go look after her, will you."

"OK," said Julie, "but there's another issue, though. There's an unconscious client in the second floor bathroom. I already called an ambulance."

"I will check it out," Mitch said. He went up to the second floor washroom and there was Darcy Hugel lying prone across the floor. Clients were showering and using the urinals and basically stepping over Darcy as he lay there. Clients were used to crazy circumstances and they had learned to just continue their business and ignore it.

The first thing Mitch did was to clear the bathroom. "Do you see this guy lying here, you knuckleheads? He might be dead for all you know."

"He can't be dead," said Richard D. "He's snoring." Richard D was another hostel regular and could be quite hilarious. Everyone in the bathroom laughed, including Mitch, but he still cleared the bathroom. The nice thing about working in a men's shelter was that guys could talk to guys like that and get away with it. Shelter guys would rebel against a female worker talking to them like that or a female client in a women's shelter would rebel against a male staff member talking to them like that. Most of these shelter clients were habitual and they knew Mitch well and even considered him one of them (because he came from where they did) in that he understood them and so they cooperated with him most of the time.

Darcy was a large man, a dockworker and had been in some major fights in and out of the shelter, even though he was rumored to be gay. There was no blood on Darcy tonight, though, and Mitch quickly assessed what had happened. A cigarette burned to the filter lay on the floor beside Darcy. What appeared to have happened was that he had been sitting with his back against the bathroom stall having a cigarette while talking to some other guys. At some point because he was too drunk to get up and go back to bed, he simply put his head down on the floor and went to sleep.

Mitch stooped down and got to within about 12 inches of Darcy and yelled, "Hey, get up." Darcy immediately opened his eyes and when he focused on Mitch, he became alarmed.

"What do you think you're doing, Darcy? You can't sleep here. Now get up or I'll get the cops to remove you and you will be barred." Darcy rose unsteadily to his feet and Mitch half supported him as he led him to his dorm bed.

Before Mitch left, he said, "Smarten up, Darcy, and don't do this again or it will be the last time."

"Sorry, Mitch, it won't happen again."

Mitch went down to cancel the ambulance that had already arrived and he dressed down Julie a little for ordering the ambulance, because it would create potential incident reports and more paperwork unnecessarily. That was the end of that episode. Comic relief was important with this kind of work and Mitch and Marcel, his back up man, created their fair share of it after incidents like that.

Morning wake-up of the clients consisted of a 6:30 a.m. buzzer and fire alarm bells ten minutes later. Breakfast was at 7:00 p.m. and everyone had to be totally cleared out of the center by 7:45 a.m. It was Marcel's job to make sure everyone was out of the dorms after the buzzer and bells went off and to lock the dorm doors after showers and breakfast at 7:45 a.m. All clients had to vacate the center at this point and although they could come back for lunch, they were not permanently allowed back into the shelter until after supper hour. That morning during general wake-up, as Marcel was flicking on dorm lights before the buzzer sounded, Marcel was having trouble waking a few difficult clients as he had been lately.

They would stay in bed and refuse to get up even after breakfast when dorms and the shelter itself were supposed to be cleared. This particular morning, Mitch went with Marcel so that they could clear the dorms more efficiently. As they were flicking the lights on in the B dorm and shouting, "time to get up, guys" through the door, they spotted big Jeff Hamish just getting dressed. He was naked and beginning to put on a pair of electric blue panty hose. Just as they came through the door, he had completed the action and had put them on. He was big and burly with a hairy chest and thick muscular legs. He looked like a deer caught in the headlights and tried to cover himself with a towel, but it was too late. Marcel and Mitch both clapped their hands to their mouths and ran from the dorm but they heard the laughter breaking out behind them from the few dorm guys who had been awake and saw the scene. They started to laugh and couldn't stop. They laughed through the rest of wake-up call; they laughed through the printing of breakfast tickets, the food line and the meds and toiletry time, right up until going home time.

Every time they would look at each other, they would laugh again. During the handing out of breakfast tickets, as the food line was moving, the laughing got so uproarious they could hardly stand up. They did not tell anyone what they were laughing at, so as not to embarrass Jeff, but he had left the center as soon as he was dressed. The laughter was infectious, though, and many clients started laughing just from seeing Mitch and Marcel laugh.

Jeff didn't return to the center for a long, long time. Mitch would go home and tell his wife of the bizarre circumstances he experienced at work and she was incredulous. Mitch's wife, Ellen, was a very nice Canadian woman of Polish descent who had sage wisdom and discernment beyond her years. When he told her things like the verbal abuse he put up with from clients or other staff calling him a curmudgeon because of his boundaries, she would say "Ignore them and continue to do what you know is right. They will realize you have a point sooner or later." She was usually right.

Don't respond in anger, you will say the wrong thing. Don't take up issues with admin or staff by e-mail or in writing because it will be misconstrued and used against you with your adversary having a living record of it. Don't offer too much info especially on controversial issues. Be very sure of someone before you tell them all that you really think; you can't take it back later. Don't indulge in gossiping; it always gets back to the person. Don't emotionally invest unless you're very sure because that person could become a dependant. In other words, help whoever you can but be careful whom you adopt.

Mitch's pet name for her was "The Godmother" and she was rarely wrong on these matters. She was the anchor; Mitch was the sail. That's what she said. It was Mitch's spiritual side that came through, however, when there was a tragedy or death in the family or spiritual direction was needed.

Chapter Two

One of their last night shifts together (before Mitch and Julie moved to full-time afternoon shifts), Marcel and Mitch experienced the battle of Thanh Lee, Bob Frost and the day of the knife fight. Bob Frost was a 220-pound, six-foot-one Caucasian who was a bit of a bully within the shelter system. He was an ironworker and a welder who had a domestic incident with his common-law wife and was going through a messy separation. Word was, though, that he had been abusive mentally, verbally and even on occasion physically. Bob wound up in a dorm with a street-smart, 38-year-old Asian man named Thanh. Bob was prejudiced and didn't like blacks or Asians. These two had already experienced a bad interaction at dinner when Bob remarked that the food that Thanh was eating was smelly. Thanh had been able to ignore his remarks thus far, however Bob's verbal attacks continued and they included vague racial remarks. The following morning in the dorm, when it became too much for Thanh to take, it all boiled over. On the morning in question, at the breakfast food line, Bob butted in line in front of Thanh and at that point, Thanh wasn't willing to take it. He said (in his broken accent), "Get out of the way, you fucking asshole."

Bob's response was, "You get out of my way, you little gook, or I will smash that tray over your fucking head."

Thanh and Bob started pushing each other until a kitchen worker broke it up. After breakfast, while Mitch was on the desk and Don M. was on duty early to relieve him (for day shift), the situation between Thanh and Bob escalated, and a fight broke out in the dorm that they were both in. Now Don M. was a large, native fellow who had rehabbed from a lifetime of alcohol and drug addiction, returned to school and become a frontline worker. Many said he was still an addict, but he was large and formidable looking and nice to have in a situation like this. One of the older dorm clients informed Mitch what had happened and he and Don went down to the dorm. When they arrived, Bob was throwing punches and Thanh had taken out his knife. After a punch to the head delivered by Bob, Thanh pulled his knife and lashed out, stabbing Bob in the abdomen. By time the knife went through his clothes, it was only a grazing wound, thankfully. Thanh immediately concealed the knife. Don tried to subdue Thanh while Mitch stepped in the middle of the two of them. They continued trying to fight over top and around Mitch until Don finally said, "Stop it you two; you're going to kill each other." Mitch was already saying, "You two are barred for three months." As he was speaking, Thanh said, "It was his fault; he called me a gook." Bob said, "This fucking china man is an idiot." Thanh threw a punch over Mitch's shoulder at Bob, just missing. Bob threw a punch back over Mitch's other shoulder and hit Thanh. Mitch held his arms out and said, "That's it. This is final; you're both barred for six months." Don rescued the knife from Thanh's jacket and both were asked to leave with their belongings.

As Mitch was waiting to leave at approximately 8:00 a.m. (after doing his incident report) and Don was preparing to take over the shift on the desk, both of them looked at the front monitor at the same time to see that the drama was continuing. In front of the facility on the surveillance camera, they saw Thanh and Bob in a full-fledged fistfight. Thanh had some karate skills that soon became apparent. Every time Bob threw a punch, Thanh could block it and return a volley of punches and kicks that could disable Bob. Thanh was taking it easy on him at this point and Bob withdrew and walked away. Thanh yelled taunting remarks after him but did not pursue him. On Monday morning, Stacey (the program director) called Mitch into a meeting. It was spread through the grapevine that Stacey was lifting Bob's barring because he was not the one with the weapon. He had gone to Stacey the day after the barring and convinced her that he was attacked and had nothing to do with confrontation. Mitch had insisted on being part of the meeting and so was called in. Stacey, as previously stated, (like others with new worker syndrome) knew nothing about real client issues or general client behavior and was all too willing to show her empathy to give someone a second chance without looking at the real issues involved. Mitch protested, "Bob, did you say anything to Thanh previous to the fight? I heard you called him a gook. Is that true?"

After a long pause, Bob said, "Well, yeah."

Then Stacey, after some prompting from the Human Resources person (Mr. Bain), finally realized what was happening and upheld the barring. She, however, never admitted that she was naive or that she could learn something from workers with experience (typical administration procedure: decisions made from above without experience, involvement, or accountability). Nor did this affect her future decisions based on unrealistic empathy and naivety to the point of not facing reality, especially as it concerned health and safety issues involving dangerous clients and the effect on other staff or clients. It would be her undoing.

Mr. Bain, one of the main H.R. people, was a long-time clergy person involved in Redemption Center—a small, bald, stocky, play-it-safe type person. His decision would have been the same as Stacey's until he heard about the racial slur; then he had to advocate for barring for Bob because of the liability involved.

When Mitch wanted to go to admin and cause a bigger stink, Mitch's wife, Godmother Ellen, said, "Lay low; stay out of it. Take a day off when you need to and wait for it to hit the fan later." As usual, she was right. It took a while but it did.

It should be said at this juncture that workers and the relationships that they develop with each other and with clients is unique and not easily understood by outsiders. Workers can be together eight to twelve hours a day, five days a week, especially if it's shift work. They may be with their co-workers more than they are with their family. Because of this and the extreme circumstances that these workers experience together, this can form a bond however platonic that is nonetheless indelible. Not that this differs extremely from other workplaces, but social workers may experience, deaths, overdoses, arrests, fights, threats, abuse and a lot of other extreme circumstances. There are also sometimes victories and even personal redemption. You could equate it to where you were and what you were doing when Kennedy was shot or during 9/11. Everyone who was alive during these events knows where they were, what they were doing, and whom they were with.

On a smaller scale, it's the same with frontline social work. Where were you when this client died? I was with my work partner, we were behind the desk, and it was a rainy night, when we found him not breathing. The police, ambulance, and coroner were eventually called. These experiences compress time. It's not like mindlessly watching TV for four hours. Every minute or hour is worth something when you're going through events of this magnitude. There is also the feeling that no one except the person or persons you experienced these things with, could possibly understand.

Families of workers don't understand how you could possibly work with this person for all those hours and then want to spend an hour on the phone with them during your time off. But it's about debriefing; it is about understanding. It is about resolution and even if none of that is accomplished immediately, it is about seeing that the other person is okay and perhaps reflecting and confirming that you're okay. Those bonds or the memory of them can last a lifetime, even when these people aren't together anymore. You can no more forget these large events in your personal history than you could a large event in world history.

These experiences are also a personal evolution. Some may become jaded, burned out, or quit, while others may gain a whole new perspective on life and even become philosophical. Once these people have been in your circle, you always wonder where their evolution led them. When it is clients, you wonder if they made it or not. Were they able to move on and better themselves? Were they able to become stable on meds, or did they overdose, go to jail or die? Being the union rep of a union local like this, you could intensify that experience times three.

Not only must you be available to advocate or defend employees with absenteeism, addictions, work performance or client complaint issues, you also must become their *Dear Abby* for personal problems.

Eventually, Julie, the 21-year-old girl whose shift Mitch followed on weekends, applied for and received the full time afternoon caseworker position. Already with two years part-time experience, a college SSW and some university courses, she was a shoo-in for the job. With members of her family already being civil servants, she was used to this kind of action and responsibility and was very mature for her age. Within four months, full-time senior employee Barry retired and Mitch decided to move to a full-time afternoon shift on the desk, which made Mitch and Julie partners.

Before Mitch had arrived, Julie had put in that long four months with Barry. Barry, who was over 65, was plain about the fact that little mattered to him at that point. He was a little old white-haired codger who wore an Indiana Jones hat and listened to ancient jazz music on Internet radio during his shift. Drunks got by him all the time. He talked on the phone while fights happened out front, people snuck in for dinner, and clients switched beds at will. He was beyond caring and Julie took the traffic, in that she was the one who had to deal with situations. She was truly happy to have Mitch as a new partner.

Meanwhile, the weekend afternoon shift for some time now consisted of Joseph B. and Eva. Joseph was 22 and Eva was 48. Eva had a tainted past and was fired from two other agencies for promiscuity and other infractions of some sort. She could be called attractive for her age but had this attitude of superiority, even though she was really quite uninformed and naively idealistic in social work. Joseph was a kid fresh out of social work school that Mitch had tried to mentor. However, although Joseph respected Mitch, he did not listen to him or anyone else for that matter. One night when Mitch was still on nights, he had come in early at approximately 11:15 p.m. Joseph was not on the desk as he should have been and Mitch could see by the surveillance camera that the case management office was closed, blinds were drawn, and the office-closed sign was on the door. Mitch phoned up, but there was no answer. After a short time, Joseph appeared at the desk, disheveled and in a sweat. Eva appeared a few minutes later, very quiet. At that point, Eva and Joseph asked Mitch if they could leave early (as a courtesy) and left together in Eva's car. Not more than a week later (when Mitch had moved to full time), Mitch was called by Stacey, the program director, to represent Joseph (as union rep) in a sexual harassment complaint sworn out by Eva.

The complete details of the whole affair were never fully disclosed but through one of Eva's closest friends, Mitch found out that Joseph and Eva had an affair (which was quite mutual) but when Eva wanted to quit, Joseph would not relent. Later, Eva proved that her behavior in this instance was a pattern with other staff and clients but at the time, it was Joseph who had to resign the Redemption Center to escape dismissal. Eva's word was unquestioned.

The first big event that happened after that on Mitch and Julie's shift was the incident involving Lester. Lester was an interesting client. He was schizophrenic and prone to some outlandish behavior but not usually violent, at least not with other people. He would lash out and punch the air and talk in an animated fashion about things that had happened to him, but he did not want to hurt anyone. Lester was also extremely intelligent and had an incredible capacity to hear, absorb, and retain information. There was not a rock band from the sixties, seventies, or eighties that he didn't know, including what songs they sang, their history and memorabilia. If you should say anything within his hearing, he would repeat it and reiterate it to you and others. He would seldom forget anything.

He created a language for himself, which was halfway between English and German but was to everyone but a few, gibberish. Lester only reverted to this language when he went off his meds and was not doing well mentally and emotionally. During these periods, Lester featured all words that had a C (or sometimes others) and changed it to a K. For example, Lester became Kystyres. Police became polikes. Bicycles and motorbikes became kyikes. When he referred to Julie, though, she was still Julie or Mitch was still Mitch.

Julie had developed a nice rapport with Lester during her part-time tenure as a caseworker. She taught him to be task oriented. He would go to the mental health clinic for his depot injection (mandatory psychotropic meds injection, court ordered as condition of parole, once a week) and meds because she would mark it on her calendar and remind him. If he did not go, she would be disappointed, and Lester wouldn't like that. If Lester wouldn't shower, she would give him a towel and ask him to shower for her. He would do it. Since she was only part time weekends, when she started this therapy, Lester would fall off during the week but when she became full time, Lester was observing these regimes on a regular basis. It was not just this that changed, either. Lester began eating at regular meal times and developing a wholesome sense of humor. Once, though, during a period when Julie was too busy to give Lester the attention he required, Lester missed his depot injection and meds appointment at the mental health clinic.

Lester began punching the air and calling down Julie for being too busy and having too many other clients and reverted to his alternate language. Julie approached him in the hallway to his room one day about these issues. "Lester, why haven't you been taking your meds, and why did you miss your appointment?"

"I can't sleep when I take those drugs," said Lester. "I drink too much coffee and smoke too many cigarettes. I'm going to run away to Toronto."

"You won't be happy there either, Lester. Stay here; this is your home, but you have to stay on your meds."

Lester began to act out. "You phoned 911 on me last time."

"Only to protect you," Julie said. Julie had cried like a baby when they took Lester away the last time in cuffs, but she had a responsibility to protect him.

This time Lester ran off. Julie and Mitch watched from the back parking lot as Lester took off like a rocket through the parking lot and down Roark Street like a jet. For a 48-year-old, this was amazing. Then when Mitch was on the desk later, he saw on the surveillance camera Lester streak across King St. West and run down Main Street. Back and forth he went until he wore himself out. Later, he could not sleep, eat, or even sit without acting out, until he himself phoned 911. Because Lester was on probation and had to take the injections as part of his order, he was permanently housed in a resident room at Redemption Center. Police showed up immediately. Lester was cuffed, arrested and taken away for his depot injection and spent a week in jail. When he was released, he was his sweet, former self.

Patrick Willis was another character much like Lester: schizophrenic also, but he had never committed a crime. Lester's crimes were not that serious either, for that matter. He had made some crank 911 calls, some vandalism, and some idle threats. Patrick was not forced to take depot injections but he was on some psychotropic oral medication, one of which was the dreaded Lithium. Patrick had some wild delusions. One of his delusions was that he thought that he could manage without his meds and that managing without his meds made him magic. He liked his delusions and illusions and to Patrick they were real. One of Patrick's illusions was that he thought that he could stand in the middle of busy Roark St. at rush hour and that traffic would obey him. He pointed to different lanes and street corners to direct traffic in this busy four-lane thoroughfare. Of course that wasn't a reality. Cars swerved around him trying to miss him, causing at least one accident and many near accidents. At some point, police witnessed this and took him in. When Patrick was released, he was medicated, and he behaved for a few weeks. Within a short time, though, he began skipping his meds again and because there were so many people to look after, sometimes workers didn't notice for a few days or even a few weeks. Soon Patrick was up to his old tricks. Another of his favorite illusions was the "Magic Door."

This was the main security door that could only be opened by the front desk attendant who could see in the camera who was at the door. He would then push a button, which would electronically open the door. Because Mitch knew Patrick, a regular room client, he would see Patrick in the camera and open the door before he ever rang the bell. This made Patrick believe that he was opening the door through his own will. He would wave his hands at the door like Count Dracula or Shazam and expect the door to open. It usually did. Around this time, Mitch developed a bit of a rapport with Patrick. He could make Patrick giggle when he called him Shazam. He could yell at Patrick for smoking in the building or picking up butts and he would sometimes listen.

On one particular day, Marcel (who was still janitor security) said to Mitch, "I'm going to come to the door ahead of Patrick and put out my arms as if I were Shazam and you open the door and then Patrick will think that I've got the magic, too." Mitch laughed and said okay. That morning before breakfast, at approximately 6:30 a.m., Patrick was out playing in traffic while Marcel was sweeping the front sidewalk. Mitch yelled out the front door, "Patrick, you silly bugger, get out of the traffic; you're going to get killed." Patrick laughed with his maniacal laugh that went up a few octaves at the end. He continued. Mitch went to the edge of the sidewalk, where Marcel had stopped sweeping. "Patrick, you're pissing me off. I'm going to call the cops. You'll get locked up again." At that point, Patrick sheepishly walked toward Mitch as cars continued to swerve around him trying to avoid him. Mitch went back to the unattended front desk. Patrick picked up a butt off the street and began to smoke it. Marcel headed into the front entrance ahead of Patrick. Patrick followed after he finished smoking his butt. Marcel made a grand show of sweeping his long winter coat out of the way and extending his hands in front of him as though lightning was about to emerge from his fingertips and he said the word *Shazam*. The door opened and Marcel walked through making eye contact with Mitch as he came up the ramp. They both restrained laughter but Marcel started to smirk a little. Patrick stood in the doorway bewildered and then walked up the ramp as though in a trance. By then, both Marcel and Mitch were behind the desk. Just as Patrick was about to pass through the main door, he said, "I'm not stupid, you know." Marcel and Mitch broke out with laughter and so did Patrick as he climbed the second floor stairs. His laughter became manic and hit the high octaves as it trailed behind him. The whole episode put Mitch in mind of that old philosophical joke concerning mental health issues.

In the 1950s, a man was driving to the country to visit relatives. But before he got out of the city, on the edge of town he got a flat tire. He pulled over and realized that his tire had gone flat directly in front of an insane asylum. There was an ominous wrought iron fence and in the second floor window, behind bars, was a wild unshaven patron, watching him. As he began to change the tire, he jacked the car up, removed the nuts from the tire, and placed them on the curb. He then replaced the tire with the spare. As he moved back, his foot accidentally kicked the nuts and they fell into the sewer. "What will I do now?" the man exclaimed as he sat on the curb exasperated. The patron in the window said, "Why don't you take one nut from each of the remaining tires and put it on the spare? Then each tire will have three nuts and you can get on your way." Incredulous, the man said, "That is so smart. What is a person with your sense doing in a place like this?" "Well," the patron answered, "I'm here because I'm crazy not because I'm stupid."

Well that's how it was for Patrick and many others who comprised that portion of the homeless population. These were the clients who had mental health issues or dual diagnosis along with addictions but were still very intelligent. That was how those clients in our system fared, not very well.

Of course, Patrick was eventually arrested for playing in traffic when he caused a two-car crash. He was put in protective custody in a smaller town where he could not get into so much trouble. Still, he was branded a criminal and he was not. There are dozens and hundreds of these unfortunates walking the street. Granted, the previous system with the old mental health facilities were archaic and restructuring was somewhat justified. But not to have mental health facilities for these people is not the answer. And every one of these unfortunates who dies, gets hurt or arrested affects the worker who tried to help, because the system doesn't work. Even though the workers in the shelter know that these people should have never been their problem and many times have caused them immeasurable extra work, they still feel remorse when they become a statistic. A study reported that six out of ten people walking the streets has some kind of mental health issue and four of them are undiagnosed. That means that six out of ten clients, workers, family, and friends have some kind of mental health issue mostly undiagnosed.

In your lifetime as a worker, you will see many of these people fall through the cracks, and tragedy and disappointment should be expected when working with these types of clients. It is the system that must change. As a worker, if you want to survive, it all boils down to not having an agenda for being a helper or being in the helping professions. New worker syndrome is common among those fresh out of college wanting to make a difference and even those administrators who have never been on the frontline—"I want to help change the world by doing anything the client asks so that all clients will love me." Wanting to be the most popular with the clients is the real reason, or from the administrator's perspective, wanting the clients to continue to use our services. They call this client-centered. It should really be called client-stupid because of all the misguided trouble it causes. When you have been in the helping professions long enough, and if you remain, you will realize that none of these are reasons to stay a helper. It is not like other positions or professions. You must be a helper because you want to help and you realize that people, from clients to workers, don't need phony friends or confidants. They need people who will tell them the truth. They don't need friends specifically; they need helpers—not enablers—helpers. When you have no more agendas and you get to this point, you've reached a plateau in your helping usefulness and in your own personal evolution.

A lot of layers need to fall off your psyche and ego before you can completely close the door on New Worker Syndrome. If you become one of these, this becomes your agenda. Those you adopt, you worry about, you think about, and you try to help them figure out the answers. This takes not just empathy but structure. It becomes the ability to teach them to manage on their own. You cry for them, you pray for them, but they can never know that. You don't emotionally invest in them but you keep them in your heart and you try to not lose a single one, if it is possible.

Chapter Three

Rick and Mitch were like uncles to Julie and very protective of her. Mitch had been Julie's partner already for five or six months before Rick came on the scene. Rick had become a placement student at Redemption Center and then a part-time employee. Rick had been through school with Julie on an upgrade after his factory days as a mature student getting an SSW (Social Service Worker) in his late forties while Julie was getting certified in her late teens. They became the most unlikely of friends, as did Julie and Mitch (who was in his fifties) on a different level. Rick and Mitch were really very much alike. They were both from union backgrounds and made the natural transition to social work after retirement or in Mitch's case, plant closure.

They both went back to school and found themselves caseworkers or residential workers in this new environment. Rick, however, had not really been around Redemption Center long enough to know Julie's capabilities as a worker or her experience as a negotiator who dealt effectively with clients. Mitch and Julie, on the other hand, were partners and shared the depth of their experiences. So the day of the mountain man incident, Rick was concerned solely about Julie's safety while Mitch tried to see the bigger picture.

When Thomas approached the desk, Mitch did worry about Julie's safety and her cavalier attitude about the situation; however, he knew she could handle it. In the homeless shelter where they worked, clients like Thomas did comprise a small percentage of the homeless population. Thomas, at first appearance, looked like an unkempt mountain man: a long, brownish gray, matted beard, long hair, six foot two inches, lumberjack coat, dirty stained blue jeans and a nasty disposition, like a junkyard dog that had been kicked too many times.

Thomas approached the security door aggressively, determined to enter. He pushed the door but it did not open. Mitch (standing in the security office) would not push the release button. Rick (still a trainee at that time) watched with amusement from an office chair. Julie was on the other side of the security glass in the lobby, only a few feet from Thomas. She spoke first, "Thomas, there have been complaints from other clients about your hygiene; you need to shower."

"No, I don't need to shower," Thomas thundered.

Mitch interjected, "We need you to do this; it's only fair to the other clients."

"I'll do it for you but not for her," Thomas replied.

"That's not very nice, Thomas. This is not personal and it's not Julie's fault," Mitch retorted. At this point Julie was suppressing a giggle and Mitch shot her a look. Rick was becoming concerned for Julie's safety (being new to the system), and even though Mitch was trying to maintain an authoritative demeanor, a smile began to twitch at the corner of his mouth.

"We are trying to help you, Thomas," Julie offered.

"Fuck you, bitch, I'm not doing anything for you," Thomas stormed again.

"Now you're barred, Thomas, and you must leave," Mitch ended. Thomas turned in anticipation of his walk down the ramp. His parting shot was to Julie, "Listen, bitch, if I ever see you on the street, I will break your fucking neck." He stormed down the ramp, never taking his eyes off them. Julie was ready to burst out laughing when Mitch mouthed the words to her and Rick, "Don't laugh."

Mitch knew that psychologically, this would rob Thomas of center stage and he would be forced to react and up the ante. Mitch, however, was on the verge of exploding with laughter himself. The second Thomas was out the door, they all erupted in laughter at the ludicrous irony of the situation and the helping professions themselves. Laughter and venting, these were the things that protected their sanity. When the laughter finally subsided, the debriefing began.

The front desk of the Redemption Center was unlike any other homeless facility. The shelter was the biggest in this region and as a result was the most fastidiously monitored. It resembled the cockpit of an airplane or a space ship. There were two large video screens with twenty-two different views from surveillance cameras dispersed strategically around the center, hallways, entrances, dining room, and exterior views. The desk was set up high, in a semi-circle and the chair was a high rolling hydraulic chair, which kept the RW (the captain of the ship) in the know, having a bird's eye view of everything.

On one of Mitch's afternoon shifts, he was working with Jodi (a young part-time staffer, who had been full-time in the past and had a wealth of experience) who was filling in a shift for Julie. Jodi was very attractive and drew male clients like flies. She was a brunette, short, only about five foot three inches but had a pretty face and was in fantastic shape, being a fitness buff. It was that night that the notorious client John Clapham decided to act up. Mitch had his problems with John C. (a permanent room resident) in the past but Mitch had a rapport with most of the guys and he could usually deal with John. On this particular shift, Mitch was on the front desk and Jodi was in case management filling in for Julie. Around 7:00 p.m., Mitch heard a scream elicited by Jodi from the second floor. Within a few seconds, Jodi had called on the walkie-talkie saying, "Look at the fucking monitor." There was John in the nude on a chair outside the case manager's office, masturbating and playing cheesecake for the camera. Mitch called the police.

They arrived within a few minutes and went up and arrested John and expedited his immediate expulsion from the building. Mitch's comment to John as he was exiting was, "Smarten up, you troublemaker, you can't do that shit here." Mitch had a way of getting to these guys. Even though he was an authority figure, he was like their dad and they knew that he did not come from a judgmental place; he simply spoke their language. John laughed at the comment. John was released within a few days but was arrested a week later for urinating on a flagpole in the city's center.

He was incarcerated for nine months but John didn't belong in jail; he should have been in a mental health facility. What Mitch wanted as a worker was a more fair system with all facets of the helping professions taking their part. Basically, mental health clients deserved mental health assistance, not a homeless shelter and not jail. The working poor and disabled did need shelters and the criminal element needed the penal system. From the clients, Mitch only expected better effort from those who had the potential or who could improve, and the least he expected from those who couldn't was to try and to have respect for him and the other staff that were trying to help them. The system, however, didn't work, which made for some understandably frustrated clients and some sad fall-through-the-cracks stories.

Stories like the sad saga of old Will were common. Old Will was one of the old residents who stayed in one of the shelter beds as a paying customer. He had outlived all his relatives and because he had some dementia and loss of memory and was 88, the Redemption Center had taken him in. Besides his dementia, Will had a huge problem with his hygiene. He wouldn't bathe or shower. In fact, he was the reason that no one wanted to stay in D dorm. And if they did, no one wanted to sleep in a bed any closer than ten or fifteen feet from Will. Finally, one time on an afternoon shift when Jodi was the caseworker (filling in for Julie again), she talked Will into going into the shower, and she got Mitch to oversee. When Jodi paged Mitch and got him down to the basement washroom, he was flabbergasted at the site of old Will naked in the shower.

Jodi handed Mitch the soap, towel, and scrub brush. "What do you want me to do with these?" Mitch said.

"Watch him shower and make sure he does it, please. I'm a girl. I can't go in there with him."

"Now you're a girl; every other time we're equal or you're the boss because you're case manager. This is what you make the big bucks for."

"Nevertheless, Mitch supervised old Will's scrubbing, and it was quite the sight—it gave Mitch nightmares for a week. Mitch was not a personal support worker nor was that in his job description. Will never stayed clean anyway and after a few days, he would smell again. He didn't wash his clothes for one thing and chewed garlic often, which was another thing.

Will smelled so bad that when you did your dorm checks at night (and entered Will's dorm) the hair stood up on the back of your neck and you got goose pimples on your arms. It was so bad that it was beyond a smell. It was like an entity. Your senses went into shock and you had a strange euphoria when you got clear of it. There was a new pump air freshener, the kind that instantly released the air freshener at intervals. It was installed in the front desk office area where there was the most traffic. It was designed to pump some air freshener every few minutes into the room to stave off odor. One day, Will approached the front desk for his meal ticket and the air freshener started pumping erratically. It made a hissing noise, the door fell open, and it sprayed a last spray and died forever. The joke around the center was that the air freshener had a heart attack.

There were times during Will's tenure at Redemption Center that he would be the sole usher for chapel on Sundays. He would pass around the basket for donations but again his odor was so bad that many times he would be asked to step aside and let someone else do it. Besides, a few times, Will would have to be told to pull his fly up because he had a tendency to not dress himself properly and he didn't wear underwear which was far too revealing for church service. Old Will eventually could not look after himself anymore and he was shipped off to an old folks' home. When the caseworkers were packing up Will's stuff and they were cutting the lock from under his bed drawer locker, they made a startling discovery. Several rows of neatly stacked bills with elastics on them were packed in the drawer. Julie swore Mitch to secrecy but the story was that the amount was $80,000. It was put into a trusteeship for Will and Will's family who would have a say on the power of attorney. Mitch guessed that other than the rent for his bed, Will spent very little and all his disability and pension checks went straight into that drawer. He told someone later that his smell was his security system because no one would approach his bed area.

Some nights, the incidents at the center took place in rapid-fire succession and although there were quieter nights, there were rarely uneventful nights. The amount of information to be processed here should give the reader some idea of the constant zoo-like atmosphere workers in this environment had to deal with.

The next week, a certain client named John Falanyi booked in on Julie and Mitch's shift. This guy was the king of the homeless scam artists and it was rumored that he had some large amounts of cash stashed. He was in a wheelchair (because of semi-paralyzed legs) even though he could walk and he had government assisted disability, CPP, and old age pension. Even though he was 65 years old, he had the ability to charm some women and scam the working poor and the homeless. He had dyed red hair; he was articulate and could play on his disability quite effectively. His latest idea was a sober house for former addicts who would work and pay rent. They could go room and board and go to AA meetings together and have counseling sessions with John as counselor, of course, even though he had no qualifications. His rationale was that being a forty-year addict (and still not clean, though he said he was) made him qualified. Because rents were expensive and that's why a lot of the working poor stayed in shelters, he soon recruited four willing candidates.

What he did was that he rented a two-bedroom apartment and divided each bedroom into two with blankets and clotheslines. He then sublet these sectioned-off parts of the apartment to other clients. He would sleep in the living room. He collected six hundred each from his renters and set up the place, which cost nothing for clotheslines and blankets, and he received donated furniture from homeless services for the cause. He spent one night in the apartment and snuck out the next day with his suitcase and $2,400 while the other clients were at work or appointments.

The guys waited faithfully for a few nights for their leader to return before they finally realized they had been scammed. When the landlord showed up for the rent, the clients didn't have it. They had given it to John, who had not paid the rent. John did this several times in several cities and to Mitch's knowledge was never caught. He would then go underground in another city for a year and begin again someplace else.

Now when the time came when Mitch finally started working with Julie full time, she already had a lot of fans among the staff and clients. She was not what you would call a worker with New Worker Syndrome. She had been around for a while and knew the score, but still had an open heart and was not jaded. She was also extremely mature for her 22 years, yet she was fun and full of mischief and liked to play games. She had a self-confidence that came from being the eldest daughter (as previously mentioned) of a family of civil servants. Although she was not beautiful in the traditional sense, she had unique quality. Her reddish brown hair was striking against her pale white skin but her ice blue eyes were not inviting and had coal steel behind them. She had heart and courage and self esteem. This was obvious because many a client fell in love with her and some staff as well, truth be known. Mitch had a protective thing happening with her, as previously stated, like an uncle. She could drive him crazy, however, with her phone calls, her boyfriends and in general, her youthful superficiality. She also got Mitch out of himself sometimes.

She could make him laugh sometimes and forget the serious side of his life. Mitch was in his fifties but was not your typical fifty-year-old. He acted young and felt young but he had the wisdom of his years. He had never, however, been privy to the experience of an adult advisor or guardian to a young woman. In fact, despite his marriage and related experience, his children nephews, neighbors, and grandchildren were mostly boys.

For the first time in his life, he was exposed to a young woman who was not a wife or a girlfriend or a relative. He adopted her as if she were a daughter or a niece. She also got a lot out of the relationship because she could ask advice, opinions, and bounce theories off a man who was old enough to be her father but was not her father but her friend. It was a unique relationship that would serve them both well and forge a longtime relationship, which others would find very confusing. Julie would do things like when Mitch was working on the computer with his arms extended she would pivot on his arms as if they were monkey bars at the park. When there was an emergency, she would grab him by the collar to discuss the emergency. If he was trying to explain a piece of music history, or a classic rock song playing on the radio (which was his passion), she would reach over and turn the volume up full and run away, or she would kick his chair to get attention while he was working, talking on the phone, or trying to talk to a fellow employee.

Mitch was no angel either, though. He would see Julie in her sandals and get a drink from the water cooler and after having his drink, he would pour the last half-cup on her feet, which would elicit a "Fuck you, Mitch." He would exploit her naivety by saying things, such as when she would say, "I'm a good person," Mitch would say, "Not bad for a superficial, spoiled brat Prima Donna." Not that Mitch really meant it but it was made to challenge her. To Mitch's surprise, however, unlike most, she could accept criticism. Mitch challenged her, made her think, and told her the truth in his view and to the best of his knowledge and she accepted that. In return, she revealed her innocence, courage, and integrity, which challenged him to be a mentor to her. This helped but it was her determination that led Julie to the place that she could complete her dream of becoming a cop, and Mitch to the place where old agendas were behind him so that he could fulfill his mission.

Still, the superficiality of youth was no joke but it was. One day, Julie was in case management and phoned Mitch at the front desk with a message. When Mitch saw the call display and that the call was internal from case management and not from outside he answered, "Yes, partner."

Julie said, "Mitch, I think my feet stink."

Mitch said, "What the hell is wrong with you?"

To Julie, it was like a national emergency. Like a little lost girl, she related, "My feet stink, Mitch. I think it's my sandals."

Mitch started laughing uproariously, which insulted Julie but also made her laugh.

Julie was due to relieve Mitch for his break, so Mitch said, "We'll check it out when you come down."

When Julie came down to relieve Mitch for break, she offered her sandals as if they were the most prized secret in the world. Mitch played along sniffing them as if this was an important mission. Mitch smelled them and threw them in the garbage can. Mitch's comment was, "Flies are falling off the ceiling with those things in the room." Julie was embarrassed, especially when Mitch told Gus (the night-shift guy) and Annette the day-shift lady and Jodi the part-timer. Sometimes to break the monotony and intensity of their work on these shifts, some of these crazy diversions were necessary.

One evening shift, when Mitch and Julie were working the 4 to 12 shift, Eva was on 2 to 6, so that the shifts overlapped. Mitch started it. He was complying with the client's request to give him shaving cream. The small little meds cup that was used for this overflowed as Mitch was pouring it and Julie said, "Sloppy." With that, Mitch unloaded a stream of shaving cream, which hit her on the arm. Eva came into the office about that time and Mitch sprayed a stream of shaving cream that landed on her arm. Eva got hold of the shaving cream and she and Julie chased Mitch out of the building, wielding the erupting shaving cream dispenser. Mitch came back into the building by the back maintenance entrance and surprised them. They jumped but Eva had the shaving cream and let a stream go right into Mitch's ear. They laughed and cleaned up.

Chapter Four

In the evolution of a nonprofit, frontline social worker, the most painful but rewarding revelation is that when you have reached the full level of your empathy and you can care without agenda, you may then realize that what you get in return is fully emotional and spiritual. It is not about money or prestige—if it is for you, then you are in the wrong business. It may seem for a time like you're getting nothing in return for your efforts: not money or appreciation from the clients or the administration. The answer is structure. Empathy without structure is self-defeating. Your clients need helpers—impartial, nonjudgmental, honest helpers—more specifically, honest with them.

In fact, it is when you get totally beyond wanting to be a superstar social worker that you see the truth about the helping professions. Trying to save the world, trying to attract people to you by helping, or by statistically being the best social worker doesn't work. It is only when you get beyond the agendas, jadedness, and self-promotion that it all begins to make sense. It is about helping each individual for success or failure, without an agenda, that then helps you to evolve and reach the next level, because in the end, helping and healing others, heals you.

Mitch was not yet at this place. He wanted to be liked by clients. He also wanted to be liked by staff, yet he ceased to think he would get a reward for it. Yet he still wanted acceptance as we all do, knowing that others thought that he was doing the right, just thing. Now the barring (or service restriction) issue, as previously mentioned, was a huge concern to staff, clients, and administrators of homeless shelters. From the staff perspective, if someone was service-restricted especially for violence, threats, theft or vandalism that person should stay barred until it was proven that this client had changed and that this behavior would not recur. This was a health and safety issue with huge liability should staff or other clients get hurt.

From the administration standpoint, it was their duty and mandate to help the homeless at whatever cost. Behind all that, though, was the pragmatic reality. From the administration's standpoint, a service-restricted person was one more bed unoccupied in the shelter. From some of the clients' perspective (the majority), they loved this mentality because it further gave them the chance to exploit the situation and the system. This was the world they had to live in and their rebellious nature was a response to it. Society-at-large was responsible and so were the frontline workers and representatives of this establishment. In short, we owed them. This represented two-thirds of the shelter system clients. This was their attitude, though only a percentage of these were demonstrative about it. The others kept silent, though unresponsive, brooding, and angry, waiting for a reason to lash out. The demeanor of these clients certainly reflected this—no greetings, no hi, bye, please, thank you, how are you—no pleasantries whatsoever. And the demands of those who were demonstrative were beyond reason. They expected free toiletries including towels, toothbrushes, razors, shampoo, laundry detergent, free clothing, three meals a day, and all the food they could carry away from the table plus a preferred bed like a lower bunk by a window.

Many clients expected these kinds of special privileges without any gratitude, responsibility, or accountability. Many times if they didn't get what they demanded, they would do something like spitting in the elevator or otherwise vandalizing the facility or staff cars or assaulting each other. These were everyday occurrences working in a homeless shelter. In most cases, these were not the elderly or those with disabilities or mental health issues but clients in their thirties, forties and fifties who simply refused to work and figured that society owed them a living. These were mostly addicts (including gamblers) or people whose families had been on assistance for years and knew no other life.

There were, however, a third of the clients who were decent human beings and legitimately fell through the cracks. With these clients, there were some rewarding and redeeming experiences. Mitch knew a reformed addict/homeless person who owned a string of car dealerships and another client who ran an addictions center that he had started after passing through the system himself. Also among the workers and student placements, some became workers or volunteers in other facilities, cops, case workers for corrections, or youth workers. Those who remembered the tutelage and help you may have offered in training them were the rewards a worker got when they mentored or helped someone of worth who made something of themselves. But it was rare.

For the moment, though, life went on that way at the shelter for a while. More and more shelter life consisted of different factions of society and the ethnic minority was represented also. These clients found themselves twice as disenfranchised as regular dorm clients. Most of these knew more about manners and respect than their Canadian counterparts ever would. They were also thankful for what they got but would not tolerate injustice or prejudice. Because of this and the respect that staff had for some of them, this made them unpopular with the regular dorm clients. This low tolerance for prejudice went double for natives.

Ben Corean was a working poor native who did not take advantage of his native status and who had always been a good client. He always left an early wake-up call, grabbed a lunch and went to work. When he needed toiletries, extra food, or a late pass, he was always respectful.

Then one day, Ben came in late after his shift (high rigging construction). He usually finished and 8:00 p.m. Today he came back at 11:15 p.m., totally hammered on booze and crack. When he could not competently walk to the desk, Mitch refused him entry. He became increasingly belligerent and confrontational and insisted on speaking to the caseworker, who that night was Mitch's regular partner Julie. Mitch would have never agreed but at that moment, Julie walked into the front desk area. Then Ben began his verbal assault centering on Julie and Mitch as representatives of the white race. He slanted his rant with the typical native rhetoric. "You fucking people stole our land."

"Ben, stop it," Mitch said. "This attitude isn't like you."

"Fuck you," Ben said. "I'll take anyone on in this fucking place. I'm going to blow this fucking place up." When any other client would approach the desk for toiletries, meds etc., Ben would threaten them or call them on. He called Mitch on, in fact. "Come out from behind that desk and I will take you on, too."

Mitch wrote a note for Julie as they were standing there to take over the conversation with Ben, hoping this would take Ben's focus off Mitch and perhaps he would settle down. Ben had said during his rant that she was the only person he could talk to. She was safe in the bubble and if the situation escalated, Mitch could slip away and call police. Ben now began to flirt with Julie in a not too flattering way, calling her baby, but he was totally focused on her. Mitch slipped away and called the police on the caseworkers' phone. Julie was saying as Mitch returned, "Ben, you have always been a good guy in here. Why are you doing this tonight? I don't understand it."

"I don't give a fuck anymore. I want to blow the whole world up and him, too," Ben said pointing to Mitch. That was it; the spell was broken and his focus was back on Mitch. Just then the police walked in and began talking to Ben who told them to beat it.

The police started by asking Ben why he was behaving this way. Ben started to cooperate and then reverted. He started by saying "I'm sorry" and then with a few more questions, his response was "fuck you." The police then began to cuff him. His last words were to Julie. "How could you do this to me, baby?" The police then dragged him from the building and charged him.

Ben's cohort, Jim Powell, returned about 12:00 a.m. and could not even walk up the stairway to the door, he was so drunk and stoned. He did not even get through the double doors; Mitch refused him entry from the intercom. So Jim tried to pick the lock on the main door with a pocketknife.

The police were called again. As soon as they appeared, Powell dropped to the ground and made himself as stiff as a rock and police had a hard time dragging him off while he was yelling, "Fuck the white man; you stole our land," the native curse to all white men, even children of Polish, Italian, Ukrainian, Spanish and other immigrants whose heritage and history had been no more pleasant than theirs and whose ancestors had been slaves and servants just like them. These were not the people who had stolen their native rights. But this was prejudice in reverse and to some natives, a white man was a white man was a white man.

Another native man, Teddy Reese, who was a very good client, would often use that as a joke later (having been witness to those scenes). After he booked in or got his toiletries, he would matter-of-factly say to Mitch, "Hey, Mitch, you stole our land."

And they would both laugh.

Chapter Five

After approximately three or four months into Mitch's full-time front desk stint, there was a placement student who came to work at Redemption Center whose name was Lou Ann. She had to do a six-month placement in both case management and on the front desk to get experience and eventually graduate. She was an incredibly nice person but lacked self-confidence and was vulnerable to criticism or rude remarks. As a placement student in case management, she had to deal with that and a lot more, not only from clients but also from other staff. The problem with low-paying frontline positions was that they were occupied by younger people trying to break into social work or nonprofits. Some of them, at times, became very competitive and even aggressive, forgetting very quickly the reason that they got into this kind of work in the first place, which was to help.

Lou's trainer said that her style was too empathetic and that she was not firm enough with clients. The administration also thought she dressed too provocatively, which was unfair considering what some of the other workers in the building wore. Lou went home in tears a few times and had a panic attack once when another staff got confrontational with her. She then worked on the desk for a few months and Mitch and Julie took her under their wings. Mitch had worked in shelters for years and was very good at maintaining boundaries with the guys and getting them to follow the rules and tow the line. Lots of clients didn't like Mitch but there were few that didn't respect him. As he had tried to explain to Lou, it wasn't about being liked, it was about helping and that sometimes meant being strict, and sometimes it meant being empathetic but it always meant maintaining equilibrium and order.

It was the same idea with the staff. Refuse to compete with them but do what you know is right with the clients and soon your worth would become apparent. Julie could appeal to their softer side sometimes, when they were angry, unreasonable or beyond reason; she could still somehow get them to comply. She would explain to them how the system worked and she was honest about when the system did not work. She explained that we were not authority figures but frontline workers. No matter what situation the staff was in, though, even if Julie thought her partner was wrong, she was always supportive to staff in front of the clients but would say something later if she disagreed. She was loyal. This is very important in frontline social work. It's like two parents who tell a child to do two different things; no wonder the child is confused or opportunistic if there is not a united front. Their styles meshed well; Julie and Mitch, as well as keeping order, could still have fun with the clients and each other.

Lou Ann flourished in this atmosphere and found her style and her confidence. One afternoon shift while she was still quite green, she was working with Mitch on the desk for part of the time and upstairs in case management with Julie the rest of the time. Mitch and Julie had a tiring, monotonous night with paperwork and details and they all had ordered Pad Thai and were stuffed afterward. Julie sat in the most comfortable chair in the front office, which was usually reserved for Mitch, and she knew that. Mitch said, "What are you doing in my chair?" Instead of arguing or doing the respectful thing and getting up, Julie said, "Take me for a ride." They both started giggling at the prospect but Lou Ann had an alarmed look on her face. Mitch grabbed the back of the chair and wheeled Julie out of the office door backward. She started giggling hysterically as they approached the long, steep ramp. Mitch was running now and the chair was rolling at breakneck speed. They approached the ramp frontward. Julie tried to stop it from going down the ramp with her feet. Then Mitch turned it around and started rolling the chair down the ramp backward. He then started running down the ramp as quickly as he could. Julie's giggling (which usually started with a couple of deep chuckles) became high-pitched laughter mixed with screaming as they sped down the ramp. Lou, manning the front desk at that point, turned red and then white. When Mitch wheeled Julie back up the ramp, he thought the ride was over. Then Julie pointed silently to a long hallway down to the discharge dorms and again they both erupted in laughter. Mitch wheeled past the client TV room on the way. The boys cheered as they went by. Lou finally started laughing as they came back into the office safely.

When Lou came into her own, she developed a comedic style all her own. The first episode was when she was invited for dinner with her new boyfriend's family and she had a terrible cold. As they were all sitting down to a nice dinner of roast beef and potatoes, she sneezed sending a green projectile into the middle of the dining room table. It was the kind of thing that could only happen to Lou, as history showed over and over again. On another occasion, she and her new boyfriend went to a provincial park, camping for the weekend. Apparently, several young people occupying the space beside them had a wild party waking her crew up and most of the other people in the park. When the park ranger and security pulled in to address the complaints, Lou Ann and her friends were questioned also. Her neighbors were ejected and banned from all provincial parks for 72 hours.

Lou could be self-righteous when it was perceived she was coming from a just position, and argued with the officers when questioned. They were trying to insinuate that because her group was near the party group that she was somewhat culpable as part of the disturbance. When Lou protested and claimed innocence, the park ranger's reply was, "I'm the park ranger and I've been doing this for a long time. I know what I'm doing so don't tell me how to do my job."

Lou's reply was "Maybe you should find another way of making a living if that's your attitude." You had to admire her heart, her humor, and her sense of justice to be that confident and rebellious if she thought it was a cause worth fighting for. Mitch credited Julie with a lot of that part of Lou's development. Still, she was a funny girl and a victim of circumstance. She was very amusing though and what Mitch admired her most for was that it never seemed to get her down. To make a long story short, Lou and her crew did get barred from all provincial parks for 72 hours also, mostly because of her chippy attitude.

Her next challenge was an encounter with a client named Jeff. Jeff was a street man in his fifties. He was enchanted by Lou and said to her that if he could think of anyone that might be a bride for him, it would be her. Lou was usually shy and understated when dealing with clients, just listening. She was learning, however, to set the boundaries and be honest with clients, herself, and other staff. Jeff had a beard and long hair going halfway down his chest and he looked like he stepped out of a Cecil B. Demille biblical classic or a member of ZZ Top. He was unkempt, unhygienic, his teeth were rotten, and he had a terrible odor, especially his breath.

When Jeff had cornered Lou and told her that she was his prospective chosen one, she very politely, after forty minutes of listening, explained to him that she had a boyfriend and that it would be against all social work rules and ethics to date him. She confided later what it would mean to her if she had to marry Jeff O'Neill. "I'd shoot myself." This was the same Lou Ann who wouldn't say a word if she were in tears six months earlier. Wow, how this job evolved people emotionally, spiritually and mentally at such an accelerated rate. She made Mitch smile and he was proud of her. Of course, trials kept coming by way of mishaps that Lou had to overcome, from the indiscretion at the dinner table to the provincial park barring or that the freakiest client in the center had a crush on her.

Well, Lou finally got her driver's license at age 24 and inherited her dad's '92 Honda, a 16-year-old car but still functional and so she got a hold of it. Her first accident was a rear-ender at a traffic light while she was not paying attention. She had bumped the rear of a pickup truck that was stopped ahead of her. Fortunately, there was no damage done and it was not reported.

No damage was done to the pickup but Lou's bumper was split in two. The second mishap was when she was backing out of her work parking lot and smashed into another car that was backing out, which knocked off her rear bumper. She had also jumped the curb at one point and dented her front fender.

Another time in her church parking lot, which was adjacent to a funeral home, her transmission was in drive when she thought it was in reverse and as a result, she smashed into the corner of the funeral home shaking the whole building. The funeral director burst from the rear door commenting to Lou, "Please have a little respect for those trying to rest in peace."

Lou eventually got full-time social work in a women's shelter and managed very well, inasmuch as she was training other workers and was considered an integral part of that team after only a very few months with that agency. She still continued to phone Mitch and Julie and they remained companions. She also continued to volunteer at Redemption Center for the time being. Basically, though, Lou had moved on and Mitch and Julie had not. They were still stuck at the Redemption Center with its archaic notions of homelessness, addictions, and mental health issues. As previously stated, the administrators of these agencies were religious figureheads promoted or installed because of religious affiliations not because of their knowledge of the job or the way the system worked. Lou Ann, for example, was considered unsuitable by the administration and if they would have had their way, she would have had to volunteer for six months before even being considered for the position of part-time employee. This is only the tip of the iceberg when considering the administration's shortsighted attitude and naivety.

To this end, there was the story of David Hoy. David was mostly blind and because of cognitive skills issues and his inability to keep doctors or social workers appointments, he had fallen through the cracks. Add to this his growing senility and his inability to care for himself (for example his incontinence) and you had a very needy client. There was no malice in David, however. He was a nice man. One day, when Julie and Mitch had a particularly trying shift, barring clients and some verbal confrontations, David broke the monotony and made them laugh.

There was a bully of a client named Mike Posey who was monopolizing the house phone. David had asked to use the phone on a few occasions and had been rebuffed by Mike. "Fuck off, old man. I'll be done when I'm done." David came to Mitch to complain, "That fucking asshole has been on the phone for two hours. What kind of place is this? I'm going for a smoke now."

"I'll deal with it," Mitch responded. Mitch went up to speak to Mike. "Mike, give me a small break, will you? There are 100 other guys in this place, and did you think someone else might want to use the phone? Have a little consideration, will you?" Mike was immediately repentant, apologized and moved off the phone. Mitch's style was probably considered unorthodox by modern social work standards, but it was effective. When David came back from his smoke, Mitch said, "David, the phone is free for you now."

"Thank you," David said. Julie was on the front desk phone talking to a friend when Mitch pointed to the surveillance monitor and started laughing.

Julie erupted in laughter also. There was the client phone unoccupied for use at a comfortable table with a comfortable chair, yet David was standing up using the pay phone. After all his complaining and bellyaching, when the phone was free he used the pay phone instead. There was no rhyme or reason for his actions. It was his senility but it was also hilarious. Julie and Mitch laughed uproariously. I'm sure by the next morning David would remember none of the night's events.

The case managers and the administration finally decided that David needed more personal support than the Redemption Center could give him. They wanted to move him to a lodging home or an old age facility. That was not what David had in mind, however. David had somehow (with the aid of a friend) gone house shopping. Besides his disability income, he had a few thousand dollars inheritance in the bank and available credit. Of course, what was best for him or others in his sphere of influence was not considered; just give him what he wants. Client-centered, they called it; client-stupid, Mitch called it or Superstar Social Worker Syndrome. Well, one day when David was touring the house he was going to buy, he slipped on the first floor stairs and fell right into the basement, through a trap door into a sub-basement. He broke his shoulder. Still, the house sale went through and the program director and the caseworker at Redemption Center condoned it. Within two months, David was found dead. After seven days in his house, he had fallen down the stairs, through the trap door and into the sub-basement and had died. His skin had turned black and the smell almost destroyed the house for future sale. David should never have been allowed to buy a house. Honesty, boundaries, and integrity were more important values than misguided empathy and false concern.

Truthfully, structure is really what most people who truly desire help want. A great mentor of Mitch's, Charlie Henman, said, "These clients don't need friends; they have lots of friends. They need helpers." Further to this thought, a client who was barred for drunk and disorderly behavior, Gary Bowles, while in the basement D dorm one night began drinking from a pop bottle filled with rum mixed with coke. Without the good common sense to go to bed, he showed up the front desk to ask for toiletries and hygiene supplies. Gus was the night guy and like Mitch had been around a long time and had some street smarts. He would help clients but he was not responsive to selfishness or childish, disrespectful behavior. When Gary showed at the front desk, he was so intoxicated and stoned (probably crack) that he was almost totally incoherent. Gus knew that he had not allowed Gary into the facility in that condition, which meant that Gary was drinking in the house, breaking two rules.

"Gary you can't stay here like that; you will have to leave."

"Fuck you, Gus. I'll do what I want; you can't kick me out." Gary had previously been in the discharge program with a broken arm and had been kicked out of there for drinking.

Rather than making him leave the facility, the discharge caseworkers had dumped him on the shelter side. Typical dumping. All social work agencies, hospitals, even police sometimes dump, regardless what they say. The game is not to look like you're dumping. Pretend you're helping the client by finding him a more appropriate place. In the case of a drunk and disorderly client, there is no appropriate place. The client then becomes someone else's problem, unless of course the client comes back. Then they empathetically and with good reason of course, dump him again. Don't get caught with him, though, or you are *it*.

When Gus told Gary to leave or he would call the police. Gary called him out of the booth to fight and said, "You come out of there and I'll kill you." When Gus said he would not, Gary's reply was, "Don't let me see you on the street or you're dead." Gus then called the police but Gary left before they arrived. The fact is there are a lot of very good reasons for dumping. The social work system is broken. There are no proper facilities or contingencies for mental health issues, addictions, rampant unemployment, the working poor, the scammers and con men, or homelessness in general. So the understaffed, over-worked frontline worker must deal with all this and the police and public services also. So when a client is not appropriate for a facility, the worker tries to make a referral to a facility or a service that might be more appropriate for the client. For example, you can't have a person with a mental health issue standing on top of their bed screaming at the top of their lungs at 3:00 a.m. stark naked when other clients are trying to sleep. You can't have a person with a raging addiction trying to negotiate a set of stairs when they are inebriated beyond reason. They could fall and cause themselves serious injury in which case the liability would be that of the facility for allowing the person to be admitted to begin with.

The answer is mental health facilities or supportive housing for those with mental health issues. There should be detox or rehab for those with chronic addictions. There should be cognitive skills and retraining for the working poor and the chronically homeless. The fact is, though, that most of these services don't exist, or when they do, they are overtaxed to capacity, or the red tape to enter into these programs is such that most clients lose steam before ever getting help. Services are overwhelmed and in the end, there is no place to send them. So the dump continues. The fact is that even if a client like Gary would have been arrested (unless he had done any real damage), he would have been released down the street or taken to another shelter.

The police couldn't possibly arrest all these people. These clients know this also and the client in question would probably be back in an hour wreaking havoc. The incident with Gary Bowles happened on Friday night. By Monday, Gary had gone crying to Stacey the PD. He was repentant and said that he was sorry and that his reaction was all based on his poor health and how he was feeling. Stacey bought it hook, line, and sinker and let him back in to the shelter. Between her and Eva, they found a way to put him back in the discharge section of the facility. Stacey lifted Gary's barring without conferring with Gus or without any resolution of better future behavior from Gary. While in discharge, he acted up again and came back to the facility totally inebriated. Mitch and Julie were on shift. Gary was refused entry and would not leave so the police were called. As the police were removing him, they gently walked him down the ramp trying to hold him up so he didn't fall. One officer had to use force in order to get him through the door because at this point, Gary was fighting. Stacey rushed down the ramp to complain that the police were being too rough on the client. The police officer told Stacey to mind her own business and let him do his job. Julie and Mitch decided to take issue with Stacey's naivety because it could cost them severely with police good will.

They asked Stacey to accompany them into an office and they spoke to her. Mitch said, "Stacey, the police did nothing wrong. They were only trying to get the client out of the building in one piece; they were not hurting him."

She admitted that they might be right and relented. Julie piped in, "We rely on the police's goodwill and if you alienate them, they will not help us, as if things here aren't bad enough already."

Well, after a couple of hours in the drunk tank, police released Gary and he returned to the center. Stacey had allowed the barring to stay lifted but Mitch phoned the HR person, Executive Director Bains. Mitch explained the situation as soon as he saw Gary in the house, and Mr. Bains reversed the decision allowing the barring to stand until they could all meet on the matter at another time. Meanwhile Gary, who had been released from jail, made a big scene at the front desk when he realized that his lifted barring had been reversed. He demanded his belongings from discharge. When Mitch went to get them, Julie came to help him. She held the garbage bags while Mitch packed the belongings. Inside the discharge office, caseworkers Eva, Stacey, and Katie T. were having a meeting. Hearing the commotion, they came out. Eva said, "What do you think you're doing?"

"Packing Gary's stuff as per the Mr. Bain's orders," Mitch said. "Gary's out front waiting for his stuff." Julie chimed in, "We cannot have him in this facility in the state he's in again." Eva did not reply. Mitch personally brought Gary's stuff out front to him and told him of his right to appeal the barring and have it reviewed by Stacey and Mr. Bains. Julie and Mitch returned to the front desk.

Before long, Eva, Stacey, and Katie T. walked by in a huff and went out into the street to Gary. In the camera, Julie and Mitch witnessed incredulously that Stacey returned a full torpedo bottle with Gary's rum and coke in it to Gary so he could continue drinking—another misguided olive branch handed out by a naive director with Superstar Social Work Syndrome.

Within two hours, she had alienated police and her staff and had empowered a client to continue his addiction and his manipulative behavior. Gary now knew that his method had worked and through this, he had empowered other clients to do the same. He had also in the process alienated and disarmed staff to provide boundaries, structure, and useful help to other clients. This was the state of the system they worked in. This was Mitch's partner Julie's last day of work. She was to become a police officer. She was passing the baton to Debbie who was in shock at what she had witnessed and what she would have to deal with as the new case manager. She was on a training shift that day. Debbie was a chubby single mom who had been on mother's assistance her whole adult life. She was 29 years old. She had returned to school to finish her course (to her credit) for frontline social work.

Chapter Six

As previously stated, just as Mitch's wife helped him plenty with her advice and opinion, Mitch helped and mentored many with his blend of Christian understanding, client experience, and years of union involvement. Many people, past and present, called for his advice and opinions and he was frequently asked to represent many in management/union disputes. In those cases not only did he count on the Lord and his wisdom but also always in his head was what the godmother would say.

At this juncture, I think the ideal of social work and non-profits for workers and management should be discussed. As previously stated, however, the ideal and the reality are two different things. The new worker in the system is full of fire and resolve to accomplish the social work ideal, help mankind. This is the ideal, not the reality, because different people get into social work for different reasons, no matter what the original ideal is. Some just need a job and can't be educated further in a different area, some want to be a superstar, some want to climb the social ladder and some genuinely want to help. All the rules, policy, procedures, and red tape make it hard to find a worker with the same mindset two years down the road that they started with. Many who started five years ago will no longer be there. They must bend the rules sometimes to help and sometimes even break the rules. The fact is (as previously stated) because the staff see so much and so many of the clients are focused exclusively on their own life, it is the staff that change mostly, not the client.

Very few clients will be success stories but the workers can't help changing forever, due to the amount of things they see and experience. Most are unaware of this, however, and remain idealistic and naive until they are overwhelmed; this is New Worker

Syndrome. This brings us to Stacey the PD. As part of her new "be more empathetic" ideal, Mitch was called into the office on a client complaint. A client had said that Mitch was rude to him. When Mitch wanted to close up the TV room at 11:00 p.m., as per policy, the client had told him to fuck off. Mitch in this case had responded in kind. The meeting was with Mr. Bain and Stacey in Bain's office. Stacey said, "I would hope with your training you would not respond like a client. You can't lose your temper with clients."

Mitch had long ago had it with Stacey and her naivety. This was a person who claimed to have twenty years experience with addictions, but the point that Mitch always made was although you may have twenty years in addictions, you don't have twenty years experience with homeless. These are not just people who've fallen through the cracks because of misfortune, mental health issues, disability, or even addictions. One-quarter to one-third of these clients are hardened criminals: guys released from jail, con men, or simply guys who don't want to work.

Empathy wasn't the total answer with clients nor could it be. Structure was important, too. These guys have lots of friends—all their street cronies. By emotionally investing, you simply put yourself on their friends list. If you get too familiar, they would inevitably ask you for money, or if you were a female, for a date or for special privileges. Whether or not you gave in, at that point you were in trouble. If you gave in or even empathetically refused, they would think of you as a mark forever. If you refused, you would be considering an authority figure who didn't understand them. It was best to keep the boundaries clear right from the beginning. Mitch was not that direct with Stacey, however. He had told her plenty of times in plenty of ways that this was not the time to pursue that argument. This was not technically disciplinary but it was a warning, and Mitch being the rep of that union local knew what that meant. Still, he was tired of playing the game and vowed to himself that he would speak the truth on this matter to the best of his ability. So Mitch's reply was, "Yeah, I lose my cool from time to time. I'm human. This client has abused and threatened me many times."

This was not an admission as to what the client had said, yet Stacey jumped on it. "You may need some training to deal with your anger."

Mitch replied, "Now you're going too far; maybe it's the system that's the problem. Have you ever really worked a shift on frontline? How would you know what it's really all about?"

Mr. Bain jumped in at this point and said, "That's enough. He understands what you're saying." The barring policy was then briefly reviewed and Mr. Bain admitted that Stacey was not being faithful to the heart of the deal in that she lifted a barring without consulting the staff who had barred the client. When Stacey wanted to continue the conversation about Mitch's demeanor with the clients, Mr. Bain finally said, "You were late for the meeting in the first place, Stacey. Mitch has to get to work and I have to go home. Enough said."

This whole episode brought to mind a biblical scripture (John 37:38) of the conversation between Jesus and Pilot. After Jesus' statement, "I am the truth," Pilot's reply was, "What is the truth?" Although that statement from Pilot was not sound when speaking to Jesus (because he had no idea who he was dealing with), it did have validity when speaking to other people. For example, it is not true that there is a Santa Claus but many people tell their two-year-olds that there is. Life is full of these kinds of gray areas. Many people also believe that their opinions on religion, politics, and personal preferences are the truth; they are not. They are only their personal opinions. How could you explain to a female boss who never worked frontline shelter work that sometimes you had to speak to the clients in their own kind of language to get respect? They wouldn't get it so you just didn't tell them. So then Stacey was one of those folks who figured she could love the bad out of the clients, always, all the time. In other words, she was an accident waiting to happen. She was the definition of the Superstar Social Worker mixed with New Worker Syndrome.

So the levels of social work went something like this: New Worker Syndrome, Client Centered, Superstar Social Worker Syndrome, Jaded but open, Jaded but closed and the final stage for the few or even one in that agency that might be left standing, the Guardian Angel Level. In the third category, the particular moniker (superstar social worker), referred to the client-centered worker who had taken that indulgence with the client to the ninth degree, which could be dangerous and scandalous. The other options, like jaded but open could allow you to work in the field for a while, though not happily. Jaded but closed would also allow you to work in the field for a while but also not happily and this would show in a cranky, no-tolerance attitude that the clients would not like. Social climber, paper pusher was also an option within this category. This allowed you to obtain a position like trustee, bookkeeper, or financial person and not have to deal with the clients much at all. If you were going to do one of these jobs, however, you could do them anywhere; it didn't have to be frontline nonprofit or social work. There are many people living through these various stages of evolution within the social work system.

"Jaded but closed" was probably the most popular. Too many workers had been in the system too long and seen too much to suddenly believe blindly anymore. It was easier to be cold and detached than to set yourself up for hurt when you experienced client betrayal, relapse, or death. "Jaded but open" was the next most popular choice because workers could still say that they were open somewhat and could relate to some clients and still be empathetic to a degree, though most of these were just an experience or two away from been jaded but closed. Mitch would say at this point that social work and frontline nonprofit are very interesting ways to make a living. You may not make a lot of money but if you survive the emotional, spiritual lessons, it is life changing. From a Christian perspective, it can make you the person you need to be. It is also, however, one of the hardest ways to make a living that you could choose.

With Stacey, the program director, it was the "Superstar Social Worker Syndrome" mixed with "New Worker Syndrome" even though she claimed to have been in the field for twenty years. Her philosophy was to help the client no matter what it cost: Make decisions for clients with mental health issues who were not regulated on meds even though she was not qualified; try to help clients get their meds when they couldn't mostly because they were addicts and had abused the system before or because their meds consisted of mostly narcotics that they were not allowed. Or she would readmit clients who had been barred for fighting or bizarre behavior. She was going to be the Florence Nightingale of the homeless and addicted. Not!

She would order her staff to book in clients (who she had not screened or screened improperly) and inevitably they would start a fight or a disturbance at 3:00 a.m., or urinate on the floor, or pull a fire alarm. This would disturb, frighten, or scare away whatever clients were in that dorm. Of course these workers didn't consider all these realities. The goal is to help the client even if it is at the detriment of ten other clients, staff, or the system at large. These client-centered pushovers are the hardest workers to retrain, to open their eyes to see the boundaries, learn to cut losses with clients, refer them to other agencies when necessary and be honest about your own and your agencies limitations. The client-centered worker will give the client whatever he wants, whenever he wants it, all the time. The rationale is, he will love me and by this I will achieve popularity and I will be considered a great worker. Wrong! It doesn't work because the client will not respect a pushover but will try to get what he can out of them and he will have learned nothing and might even be worse for the experience.

Other staff will dislike you because you will be the one who gives the clients all the breaks and they will be the ones who have to say no because they are experienced and know the boundaries. In the end, you won't be able to keep the clients happy anyway because there will come a time when you have to say no, inevitably. If you don't ever say no, clients will continue to take advantage and eventually they will cross the line sometimes to the extreme when they ask you for personal attention, money, or other special privileges. Just like New Worker Syndrome, client-centered doesn't work either. The social climber, pencil pusher sometimes works. You will have to have a cold detached individual who is not too tolerant of the frontline system anymore but does good paperwork, keeps statistics well, and follows procedure. In other words, they can take care of the financial end. This allows this person to not have to deal too much, with the frontline system. They bury themselves in statistical systems and philosophize about why things are as they are but never invest in clients and ignore the stories they hear—very unfulfilling and many leave these positions, also. The end of this evolution usually requires many years of change if the worker stays in the field. Whether or not the general public understands it, the helping professions are supposed to be a Christian concept. What they have evolved into is mostly not. On rare occasions, however, for the rare individual it does happen. A person can come to a place when they've paid their dues and overcome the early stages of being a worker.

If they are there for the same reason they came into the field—to help—they can reach a level of equilibrium. Mitch would call it the Guardian Angel Level because even though people are not literally guardian angels, they have become helpers without agenda. They are not just helpers but mentors to clients and staff also. Another Christian concept comes into play here. Suffering refines the spirit. When you have passed through these stages, you are ready to teach others. Once in awhile, you will mentor placement students or other younger staff or the rare client who seriously wants to change. Then you truly do become a hero or superstar if only to just that one. Then someone says, "Thank you; your influence helped me to change." This is actually the most satisfying part of social work and why most people get into the field in the first place but which most never experience. We can take a lot of abuse from clients at different times, which causes some bitter feelings and until we get to the point where we can accept that as part of the territory and still be comfortable in our own skin and not thinking of retribution even mentally, we may find some inner peace with this sort of work. In the atmosphere of the new frontline social work situation, though, accountability is the key as with any other sector of the work world. This was the new world situation and as such, frontline social work now consisted of recording and reporting every minor event to further complicate an almost impossible task for staff. Surveillance cameras were now also placed in the front desk area and in the caseworker's office as well as all public areas in and around the building. Workers when dealing with clients expected statistics and accountability at all times, but as far as debriefing, EAP or extra staff for stressed-out workers, there was none. Clients who were drunk or barred and could not be admitted had to be referred to other shelters who would not admit them either. Then police would be called and reports would need to be made. Police would drop them off down the street and they would be back making a nuisance of themselves within an hour until they were finally taken away permanently or the person running the shelter at that time would make the decision to keep them. This was another administrative decision from an administrator that had no clue about frontline.

Take the tale of William Hobson, who had no legs and was in a wheelchair but was an abusive, confrontational alcoholic. No shelter in the city would take him except Redemption Center. He was verbally abusive, habitually drunk, and incontinent. When he was drunk, he could be very violent, throwing food trays and other objects at staff and clients to make up for the suffering from his disability, according to the public health worker. We said he was willful and manipulative. These attitudes also saved them having to work with William to get on treatment and eventually get into a hospice. Instead they could leave him with Redemption Center Staff. There inevitably came a time when even police were fed up with him.

One night they dropped him out front of the center in a totally drunken state. This was at 2:00 a.m., after the front doors were locked. He banged and screamed at the door but the night worker Gus would not open it. After exhausting himself, William went across the street into the shadow of the town arena and started to drink his mickie of vodka, not that he needed anymore. He then pulled a stunt sure to get attention and get Gus in trouble. He got out of his wheelchair and began dragging himself across the street on his hands, his leg stumps dragging behind. Gus still did not let him in. An outside party who picked

William up and took him away called police. Somehow the director, Stacey, was informed of the incident and called to view the surveillance camera in the morning. Of course, it was Gus who got in trouble for not being empathetic and being unsupportive of a client in crisis. The truth was that Robson was not in crisis at all. He was drunk. He could have accessed the shelter at any time during the evening but he chose to drink first, missed 11:00 p.m. curfew and returned after 2:00 a.m., totally inebriated. His behavior, then, was attention seeking and all designed to get his own way. Gus was not stupid enough to fall for it; neither were the police. They had too much experience with alcohol and other addictions and with William specifically. Of course, the administration under Stacey bought into it hook, line, and sinker and went to find William to offer him the hospitality of the center in empathy for his plight and allowed William in again. On his first night back, he was drunk and disorderly, started a fight, and urinated on the floor. He was escorted out by police and eventually taken to detox, rehab, and a lodging home at which he lasted a month.

Len Goodwall was another client just as attention seeking but with one leg missing and in a wheelchair. When he couldn't get as many hydro morphine pills as he wanted (because he was meds seeking and an alcoholic), he threw himself out of his wheelchair and down a flight of stairs so that he could be sent to the hospital and get his painkillers.

As frontline staff was always telling administration, this was not unusual behavior from clients. This was not Disneyland. If the administration wanted to be more lax with letting in drunks, addicts, and those with mental health issues (not on meds) or those who were barred for violence, then they would have to provide extra staff, some specialized staff, and possibly even security.

Mike Taft was the client who started the ball rolling. He was a big street bully who dominated most other clients, which empowered him and made him think he could do whatever he wanted. He started flirting with the caseworker Debbie (who would eventually replace Julie as full-time staff and Mitch's partner) as she was serving snack to the guys. When she would not cooperate, he insulted her by calling her a fat cunt and he began physically touching her on her shoulders and back. Finally, she protested and barred him for a month. Debbie was a single mom who had gone back to school and got a social work certificate. She was attractive in a way and attracted clients, though she was very overweight.

Mike Taft, at that point (if you can believe the audacity) went to Stacey during daytime hours to protest his barring and say that it was unjust. Stacey called a meeting. Stacey and the manager asked Debbie to lift the barring and Debbie complied. This, however, opened a whole can of beans as far as staff safety was concerned and although Taft was not a further problem, the whole shelter system became a volatile powder keg because of the administration's decision. Staff was also now allowed only to bar clients for twenty-four hours, to be reviewed by a manager or PD. The lack of consequences that this offered to some clients and the position that this put staff in was unimaginable. Ability to refuse work based on dangerous clients became a huge issue in the months and years to come and continues to be to this day.

As we leave this section and move into the next sections of this book, we will follow the evolution of the characters, their methods, the system, and the results of all this in human terms. There might be some observations thus far, though, that make sense. One client, David Hoy, died. He died because misguided workers gave him what he wanted even though what he wanted was not good for him. If he could manage on his own, he would have never been in a lodging home to begin with. John Clapham was locked up in jail for his lewd act rather than being treated at a mental facility, even though he had a documented case of schizophrenia. Worker Debbie was abused and traumatized and eventually left casework and the client was given a slap on the wrist and allowed back into the shelter. This is all "New Worker Syndrome" from the authorities, the workers, and the administration of the shelter. No one should get into frontline social work or a nonprofit because they need any kind of job or because they want to climb the social ladder or be a star. It's not a Fortune 500 company. This thing is about helping people and it's not about adulation. You help because you are here to help. You should not expect accolades from anyone, even the client or person you helped. Sometimes, it's better they don't know. You do it because it's the right thing to do and it goes on that personal slate inside you. As the Scripture says: "Do not do acts of charity or mercy to be seen but do them in secret and the Lord will reward you openly."

PART II: Client Centered

Chapter One

Before we address the client-centered phenomenon that is so popular among workers, we should discuss the policies and procedures and codes of ethics that are part of every aspect of worker-client relations. Every province has a social work college, which has a general code of ethics that is not just provincial but municipal and federal. Just like the college of nurses, these governing bodies set down rules and boundaries, which they expect their graduates and workers to follow. These workers are expected to be sanctioned by the college of social workers though this is not a hard and fast rule when hiring for frontline workers. The reason is that a frontline worker who is breaking up fights, giving out towels, unplugging toilets, and doing rounds would not stay a frontline worker very long if they had a degree or certificate. This sanctioning is mostly for caseworkers and upper management but even then, not all of these are sanctioned or educationally qualified. In addition to these codes of ethics, most agencies have their own policies and procedures, which usually are focused on their mission statement and their religious and moral orientation. Some standard policies, procedures, and rules of behavior are also in force. Mitch had been in this business for many years and he had seen it all: staff having affairs with other staff, administration having affairs with staff, religious figureheads having affairs with staff, administration having affairs with clients. And this was just the promiscuity aspect not to mention theft, drug use, and other offences. Mitch had seen every configuration of human aberration within the helping professions and nothing surprised him anymore. Of all these things he had witnessed, he had never seen a staff or an administrator or a religious figurehead who was prosecuted. The bottom line was that policies and procedures and codes of ethics were not the law. The fact was that these people were not criminals generally. A staff, administrator, client, or even a religious figurehead could be reassigned, censured, or terminated for such behavior but they could not usually be prosecuted. Life was a messy business in every sector of society and social work was no different. In fact, social work was probably messier than most. You couldn't tell someone they couldn't fall in love with someone else whoever they were. You couldn't tell someone that they couldn't fall off the wagon and have an addictions problem or a financial problem or a boundary issue. The truth was that many workers and as well as clients had these issues. And although administration came down hard on those found guilty of these infractions, in many cases, they were just as guilty themselves. Although it's not widely spoken of, people are people and these issues happen in every sector of society. Proud judgment is certainly not the way to solve these issues. From a religious aspect, some of the people that administrate these agencies are what some Christians might call Pharisees. They love to judge others but not themselves.

From the social work perspective, part of the problem is that young people fresh out of school have replaced more experienced caseworkers and administrators. They may have degrees and letters after their names but in terms of practical experience, they are lost in the world of streetwise clients. Part of the problem is that a lot of men don't sign up for social work courses; 84 percent of new graduates from social work courses are female. Even the males are usually young and very inexperienced. So you might have a twenty-year-old female giving advice to male clients in their forties and fifties and trying to tell them what is the successful way to get their life on course. Empathy beyond sense is the new direction and although clients may play along to receive the assistance they need, it's mostly a joke to them. How could someone younger than most of their children give them life advice when they have not yet experienced life?

Most of the administrators also are older females with degrees who primarily like to hire females and young people. Of the four main men's shelters and several satellite services (including women's shelters) in test city, all except for one had a female director and executive director. Men were not considered empathetic enough to be effective administrators by this inner circle of administrators. Actually, a male could not even be a janitor at a women's facility. Men were strictly taboo in these services, yet women ran all of the men's services.

Mitch was a witness to the fact that women in power could be as bad as men and sometimes worse. Within the '90s and the early 2000s, this group of women had all but ferreted out the older male counselors with years of natural experience (in addictions and male cognitive and emotional problems) and replaced them all with young girls or generation x, non-threatening, computer geek males. Behind the scenes (by clients and some male staff), this inner circle of female administrators was called the femme-Nazi gang.

You didn't want to get on the wrong side of this femme-Nazi crew, especially if you were male. If they wanted to get rid of you, they would, and gossip, false accusations, and innuendo were not beyond the tools they would use. This was the larger faction that ran the city and administrated social work to the agencies.

The director of this unit was a five-foot woman named Tammy Jean (The Little Napoleon). Her inner circle consisted of Jessie Ann (a caseworker) and a nurse, Christine. Many of the girls and women that they hired screwed up just as badly as the males and in a few cases worse than almost anything Mitch had ever seen. Yet it took a long time to get rid of any of them. Stacey, as earlier stated, was the program director for Mitch's particular agency and Julie about that time was getting ready to leave the agency to become a cop. Although Stacey and her comrades were just as far off the wall with their thinking and policies as the big girls, that's where the similarity ended. Stacey was no femme-Nazi. In fact, she may have liked men a little too much. She was different in that fundamental way. She was totally female in her attire and her thinking. You might even call her tacky with the gaudy short dresses, too much eye makeup, and too much lipstick painted on to the point that the liner was above her lips to make her lips look bigger. She was also very flirty with clients and staff. She also had an addiction problem, mostly abuse of prescription medication. She seemed high all the time. She would fall asleep at meetings and phase out during conversations. Until these issues became beyond control, however, the administration would not recognize them. Staff's word, opinions, or suggestions were considered by administration to be a joke. Even when an issue was proved to be factual, there was no admission of guilt.

The administration continued to do exactly as it pleased usually saying a prayer after the fact as a failsafe rather than praying before taking up an issue and waiting for direction or guidance on a decision. Case in point was Eva the caseworker. This is the same Eva who a year and a half earlier had been caught with Joseph B., the kid, and accused him of sexual harassment when they had openly been fooling around for months. Mitch knew it was rumored that she was having an affair with a client at present. The two of them had been seen by other workers and clients out drinking together and meeting with other clients. When Stacey, the director, had been informed of this, she simply pooh-poohed it. It was then noticed by staff working nights and afternoons, that Stacey, Eva, nurse Christine, and a few other female staff were leaving their cars in the parking lot after their day shift and returning (to pick them up) at some very late hours usually inebriated, sometimes to the point of not being able to walk too well.

This began to happen more and more often. Many a client talked about seeing these ladies at the hotel and even singing karaoke after having a few. Still, the mostly female administration with the typical male religious figurehead would do nothing about the situation. Even when there was a surveillance video of Stacey, the director, doing cheesecake poses in a mini-dress on the hood of her car while clients stood around watching, the administration did nothing. Julie, Mitch, and new caseworker Debbie were incredulous at it all. Without prejudice, it must be said (and was even said by many a female staff), if a male were guilty of similar behavior, he would have been fired a long time ago. This atmosphere continued for quite some time, while other staff were being berated or disciplined for minor infractions like lack of empathy toward clients or not subscribing to Stacey's program. Stacey mostly administrated this vendetta with the help of her little group of gossiping comrades. This was the local faction of the femme-Nazi crew, which had very little to do with the higher-level faction. And things pretty well continued that way until Blain H. came along. Blain was a client with an addictions issue (crack, alcohol, and other drugs). He couldn't seem to make any progress with any of the caseworkers, mostly because he wouldn't do what he was asked. He was noncompliant. Instead of accepting that and listening to the workers, he went to complain to Stacey. Unbelievably, she listened to him, believed him, and became his personal counselor, which was totally outside of her role and a slap in the face to the other caseworkers. That was the beginning of the story of Blain and Stacey. To be continued . . .

Being the union rep in this atmosphere was very difficult. Staff was always mad at the administration and the administration couldn't care less. They didn't care if you complained. They didn't care if you quit. They didn't care if you got fired. The only thing they did claim to care about was the clients. They didn't even care about that, however. They never had to deal with client issues because they had frontline staff to do that, but when it came to resolving these issues, they did it only from their mission outlook.

Clients always got the benefit of the doubt and staff always had to defend themselves. The administration would do anything to look right in the public eye to keep that provincial funding coming in, not to mention the donations and the free press. And the clients took opportunistic full advantage of the situation and loved it.

Meanwhile (while Julie was still there), Julie and Mitch had to deal with most things mostly on their own without Stacey because they knew that she would only complicate problems in most situations: Case in point, the Angus McRay and Jimmy Harris incident. This was the atmosphere that Julie and Mitch found themselves in the night of the big battle. Angus was a longtime homeless, alcoholic, brawling Irishman. Even though his mother was a cop, he had been in trouble his whole life. He had been to jail several times for assaults and was proud of it and of his lifestyle. Jimmy was fairly new in the house; he had only been in a week. He was a drinker and a crack head also. When Jimmy was drunk and someone said anything that he perceived questionable or insulting, he would simply punch them in the face. He usually knocked the person down because it was usually an older disabled or defenseless person. He would punch them and walk away.

On this particular night when Mitch and Julie were on duty, Jimmy had been signed into the C dorm with Angus. Angus was not in for the night yet, so Jimmy started settling himself in. This was some time before the bag searches became policy at the center and Jimmy had a bottle in his bag. He started drinking up in the dorm early. To complicate matters, Dan McGee, also a notorious crack user and drinker, had a room now adjacent to the C dorm that Jimmy was in. He was already drinking also and smoking a joint with his door open.

Mitch was in the front office booking in clients but keeping an eye on the monitors. Julie was up in the caseworker's office seeing clients and answering phone calls. From viewing the front desk monitors later and talking to clients, it started somewhat like this: Jimmy was walking by the door of Dan McGee's room when the smell of pot attracted Jimmy. Dan invited him in for a drink and a toke. Jimmy went into the room and they began drinking from the bottle and doing a joint when Jimmy said, "This room stinks like dirty socks. Why don't you clean it up and stop being a pig?" Dan said, "Go fuck yourself and get out." Jimmy then punched Dan, grabbed the bag of pot, and ran from the room. The next thing Mitch knew, Julie was yelling from the top of the stairs, "Mitch, come up here and help me." Clients were also saying, "Better hurry up." Mitch ran up the stairs to find Dan's room still open and a spilled bottle on the ground with what looked to be cooking wine. There was also an ugly gash over Dan's eye. Even though the camera would later show that Jimmy did enter the room so did a lot of other people. It was therefore not conclusive that Jimmy punched him. When Mitch entered the dorm and asked Jimmy, of course his reply was, "I never touched that guy, man; he's nuts and he's drunk and stoned." Mitch replied, "Well you're drunk and stoned, too. "No I'm not," said Jimmy. "I had a few when I went out but that was it." Jimmy was much more coherent than Dan, so Dan was ejected for the night and Jimmy was allowed to stay.

Getting rid of Danny when he was drunk was never fun. Julie watched the desk while Mitch went up to deal with the situation. Dan started the old song and dance. "This is the place where I live. It's my home. You can't kick me out. Where can I go?" Danny could hardly dress himself and was refusing to go, so Julie had to call the police. He went out in cuffs, ranting and raving but even the leverage we gave him by not barring him was not good enough. He was allowed in by the administration the next day. As for Jimmy, unbeknownst to us (as it was a very busy night), he continued to drink up in his dorm. Angus had worked late and went for quite a few after work. This was approximately 9 p.m. and Julie and Mitch were having their break on the desk while still keeping an eye on things. Julie had just returned to her office when all hell broke loose Angus started up the stairs to the center when Jimmy was on his way out for a smoke. Jimmy asked Angus, "Do you have any crack?" "No," Angus replied, "I don't have any crack because I'm not a crack head." This was the perfect remark for one of Jimmy's one-punch wonder routines. He picked the wrong guy this time though. He threw the sucker punch at Angus and it was a good one; it knocked Angus down. While Jimmy was still reveling in his punch, Angus got up in a shot. He pushed Jimmy right down the stairs where he was and started wailing away on him with his fists.

Mitch began yelling from the office, "Stop that," but Angus continued. Every time Jimmy tried to get up, Angus would push him down again. Eventually Jimmy was able to crawl down by the other entrance and what he did was put his coat over his head and try to cover himself. By this time, there were several people watching. Clients didn't want to get involved so they wouldn't come into the building. Instead, they gathered out front and watched through the window. Other clients were also watching from several different doors and windows within the building. About this time, Mitch called Julie on the phone. "You better get down here; there is a big fight going on and I need you."

Julie never questioned or asked what's going on, as some would have. She knew if Mitch was that serious, something was going on. "I'll be right down," was her reply.

Meanwhile in the entrance, the fight continued to play to a growing audience, which was quickly becoming a capacity crowd. Angus began kicking Jimmy in the head while he was talking to him. Mitch left the desk as Julie was coming down the stairs and he asked her to watch the phone and the desk. Mitch opened the door to the main entrance after clearing the crowd from in front of it and began to try to speak to Angus. Angus continued kicking and talking. He was saying to Jimmy, "Okay, hot shot, you had enough now?" He kicked a few more times quite hard to make sure the message was received. Angus is not what you would have called a big man but he was tall and gangly and he had big work-worn hands. He wore construction boots all the time. He even went to bed with them on and this is what he was using to kick Jimmy with. Mitch tried to interject and said to Angus, "Stop it, Angus, you're going to kill him. You're going to wind up in jail. Is it worth it?" "I don't give a fuck," said Angus. "He started it, he punched me for nothing and he's a drug dealing pain in the ass anyway, ask anyone." Angus had continued kicking throughout the conversation when suddenly Jimmy stuck his head out from under the coat in reply to Angus's question of have you had enough. Jimmy's reply was "Fuck you, goof" and ducked back under the coat. At that, Angus re-doubled his efforts and kicked a frenzy of kicks at Jimmy's head.

It was starting to look as if no one could stop this in time and that Jimmy might die. Mitch ran back to the front desk area to confer with Julie. Julie had already called police 911 and they were on their way. Julie asked if she should try talking to them and Mitch replied, "If you think you can do any good." When Julie appeared at the other doorway entrance, her appearance and her voice made Angus stop for a minute. "Angus, stop, or you're going to get barred from here and wind up in jail; just stop it." Angus continued. Julie shrieked, "Stop it, you're killing him." Angus continued kicking. "I don't care if I kill him—he's an asshole."

Just then, the police pulled up, sirens blaring. Angus took a few more kicks when he saw them coming. As they were cuffing him and pulling him away, he said, "I was just defending myself." Jimmy popped up from under the coat claiming he wasn't hurt but you could see that his nose was flattened and there was blood coming out of it. He was red and bruised all over. They told him he was barred, also, but even though they did bar him, Stacey let him back in the next day because she claimed he was the victim. The administration disputed it. Julie, Mitch, and even Mr. Bain agreed, especially after viewing the videotape. Later on the same evening of the incident, the phone rang on the desk and it was Angus. He had already been released from jail. He knew he was barred and he knew there was no reason to talk to Mitch because he couldn't change anything anyway.

As previously stated, Mitch with all his crankiness did have empathy but he expected structure also and an effort and boundaries. He accepted the clients for what they were but he expected them to be honest about it and try. Some of them considered him their dad. So Angus asked the question of Mitch, "Well did I do good; are you proud of me? See what I did to that idiot."

Mitch's response disappointed Angus. "It's not the answer to anything, Angus. It doesn't prove a thing. He's the same as he was before and so are you and you're the one that's going to pay for the assault. Why don't you try using your brains instead of your fists, sometimes? You know you're barred," Mitch said "so take it up with the administration if you want to get it lifted."

"So you hate me now."

Mitch's reply was, "It's quite the opposite. You have a lot of potential but I can't accept you wasting it like this."

"Now you sound like my mom. I don't want to hear no more. I want to talk to Julie; maybe she'll understand."

The response from Julie, however, was not much different than Mitch's. In fact, her comment was that she found it disgusting. That was the last they saw of Angus or Jimmy for a while, but it left them somewhat melancholy: a person with so much potential reduced to what he was and proud of it. It's how he learned to survive and no one was going to judge him on it, right or wrong. He was a soul beyond our help for now but maybe not a total write off, not yet. All you could do was pray.

Chapter Two

About this time, a lot of employees seemed to be getting in trouble for absenteeism, losing it with clients, and being unable to properly fulfill the job description as set before them. It was an unjust and unfair job description to begin with. Previous to Stacey coming on as program director, the staff was without leadership for almost a year. Although Mitch wasn't a witness to it, the previous administration was supposedly as bad as this one. In either case, considering the added number of clients, the same skeleton staff, and the lack of cooperation when it came to disciplining clients by administration (and the administration incompetence itself not to mention the shifts), it just seemed too much for most employees to handle. Absenteeism seemed a natural solution for employees and from the union standpoint, Mitch defended this absenteeism somewhat vigorously, mostly because there was no debriefing, understanding, or counseling for employees and their problems, just for clients. If the administration wanted to solve these problems diligently, they would try to help the staff as well as the clients rather than ignoring the complaints and allowing the situation to fester. The upper administration (or the city) was no better. When a client wanted to go to a city worker, they had to visit the provincial office. There were armed guards at the doors and within the interview front desk area. If a client even raised his voice to a city worker, he was whisked out of the building. Yet the same administrators had little or no empathy when it came to far worse conditions in the shelters with minimal staff dealing with alcoholics, addictions, mental health, and security issues. All staff complaints were pooh-poohed.

Debbie and Mitch had already started settling in as partners within a month of Julie leaving the center. Debbie also became popular with clients but she also quickly learned that most of them have an agenda. She had already had the incident with Mike Taft (and the sexual assault) and also understood the unwillingness of the administration to back up their employees. Mitch had appointed Debbie the other union steward, which was his right to do as the union rep and being that there was a vacancy. Debbie and Stacey began to butt heads immediately. Debbie was not allowed to run special events. She was not allowed a budget for treats for the guys during movie nights. She was rarely recompensed for movies that she rented or borrowed. Debbie was very confrontational also and she had Stacey's number, in that she knew that Stacey sought attention and that her client-centered approach was all meant to make herself popular.

Stacey also didn't want Debbie interacting too much with the clients. Stacey didn't like the fact that Debbie would come and help Mitch during the food line to distribute tickets and process people through. She had never complained about this when Julie was Mitch's partner, which just upset Debbie more. Debbie continued to spend time on the desk during the dinner hour until Stacey finally confronted her. Stacey started by saying, "Are you down here again at dinner? You're supposed to be up in the caseworker's office." She had said this right in front of the clients who were standing there waiting for dinner tickets. Debbie blew up and said, "That is what all caseworkers do. They help out on the desk during the busy time of dinner hour and then make rounds down in the cafeteria and then go up to the caseworker office after 5:00 p.m. Are you not aware of these policies?" Debbie stated, "You're supposed to be the program director."

At this point, Stacey motioned Debbie toward the med's room, which was a small little closet-like room where meds were kept for the clients. They went in and closed the door. Closing the door didn't help much, though, because all the clients and Mitch who was running the desk at that time could hear every word.

"You can't talk to me like that, Debbie. You are my subordinate. I'm supposed to be your superior. What you are doing is rude and disrespectful. I'm going to write you up for insubordination."

Voices were raised to a fever pitch and Debbie made no bones about the way she felt. "You started it," said Debbie, "right in front of the clients. You demeaned me. What did you expect me to do? Besides the fact, you have been picking on me since I started here. Eva and you and all the others can go where you want and do whatever you want but I've got to watch everything I do. It hardly seems fair." Stacey ended the conversation there and said, "We will be meeting with Mr. Bain and also Mr. Watson in the office tomorrow."

Mr. Watson was the new executive director of the center (while Mr. Bain was the background HR guy with all the power). He had started out being a very nice guy then quickly turned into a little Hitler. He was the same as all the rest now.

The administration told Mitch that he would have to represent Debbie at a meeting the next day and there were two others on the roster from the desk, Annette and Rita, both were being called in for absenteeism. Mitch had one at 1:00 p.m., one at 2:00 p.m., and one at 3:00 p.m. Tomorrow wasn't going to be a very nice day. Annette was the caustic, no-nonsense matriarch of the desk who had many years experience, while Rita was her heir apparent except that Rita was three times more outspoken.

Well tomorrow came and it wasn't as bad as Mitch had anticipated. Rita and Annette both got off on a technicality, which was that the particular week that they went through was so stressful that they both needed a mental health day. Although Stacey protested, Mr. Watson and Mr. Bain were both for having the written warnings reduced to letters of concern, which would not go in the employee's file. In other words, there was no disciplinary action. Debbie's case was a little different. It wasn't just that she was supposedly insubordinate to Stacey; it was that she refused to do what Stacey told her. Mr. Bain, Mr. Watson, and Stacey had planned a written warning, which was a first step toward dismissal for Debbie. Mitch's comment to Stacey was that she really didn't know what it was like to work on the front desk.

The supper hour was the busiest time of the day. Help was required and traditionally, the caseworker had always been the one who chipped in when she was not too busy. "But Debbie's attitude toward me in front of the clients is not acceptable," said Stacey. Mr. Watson chimed in and said that he was not aware that caseworkers traditionally helped on the desk. "I would be willing to reduce this from a written warning to a verbal warning," said Mr. Watson. "I would agree," said Mr. Bain. Stacey did not agree and neither did Debbie for that matter. Debbie thought that Stacey was unreasonable and she had every right to challenge her orders, which she felt made no sense. You don't talk to your supervisor like that in front of staff and clients, however. They all settled for the verbal warning. Debbie eventually understood the reasons why but Stacey harbored a grudge that she was bound to fulfill sooner or later.

Mitch was somewhat upset by the ingratitude of some of the staff that he defended. He himself was always under the watchful eye of the administration because of his union affiliations, yet it seemed the staff themselves appreciated very little the fact that many of them would be without a job if it were not for the union. Whether their original disciplines were reduced or removed, the union did help to keep their jobs and fight for their rights. When Mitch went home and discussed all this with the godmother, the godmother's advice was sound as usual. "All people are fallible. Who can you trust completely; is there anyone? Does it matter what anyone says anyway as long as you know what you did was right?"

This brings us to the subject of friends and mentors. How many friends do you have that would stick with you through controversial times or crisis situations? How many would abandon you when you need a shoulder to cry on? Most people are so needy themselves that when you do wind up telling them your problems, you end up comforting them. Very few people are true friends or helpers or possess the stability, wisdom, and spiritual equilibrium to truly be helpful.

When it came to mentors or friends of old that Mitch had met, very few were true. Mitch had some good friends and he trusted a few very select people, however all people are fallible and he had found no one a perfect example, except for his belief and faith in Christ. Mentors generally like to raise people up through the ranks and show them the ropes so that eventually, they can do the work and the mentor can sit back and orchestrate like a puppet master.

It usually comes down to a matter of idealism versus dollars and cents, however, or the approval of upper management. When this is the choice, the dollars and cents wins every time. No matter how idealistic they may seem from the outside, when it comes down to a threat to their livelihood, it's going to be the other person who is sacrificed, not them. Mitch found this to be true in every case and it still is today. Absolute power corrupts absolutely, unless you have the Lord. The Comforter or the Spirit is the only thing that keeps your conscience true. It is the only answer and the only thing that works. The true Christian does not work through attrition but the opposite. Through a true heart of helping and giving to the edification and fulfillment of another through the salvation of another, their edict is fulfilled.

About this time, there was a client named Ralph who suffered from a myriad of problems including severe heart issues, poor circulation, and chronic high blood pressure. He was a client of Debbie's and both she and Mitch liked him. He was friendly, he was decent, and you could have a meaningful conversation with him. Well one night, he didn't come for his night meds. A strange odor was emanating from the part of the building where his room was so Debbie decided to check on him. Ralph was dead. Eva, who was his worker, should have checked on him first thing in the morning but she did not. As a result, he died and lay there for twelve hours. Mitch and Debbie discovered him around 10:00 p.m. This meant calling in Mr. Watson and Program Director Stacey, also the coroner and the police. Reports needed to be made and they were all there far after-hours. When Mr. Watson and his wife, Kim, (who was a chaplain) came in to the workplace, they spoke to Debbie, who was quite distraught. They spent a few minutes trying to comfort her; however, there was no formal debriefing as there should be in these agencies and in these situations. They finally watched Ralph being wheeled away on a stretcher and business went on as usual at the desk as if nothing had happened except Debbie and Mitch knew different. This way of making a living could be very hurtful and grieving was done on your own time, not on company time.

About this time, the HR person, Mr. Bain, decided to spend some grant money on improving the center. Their plan was to put in new washrooms throughout the old building—the best that money could buy—stainless steel. After the washrooms went over budget, partly because asbestos had to be removed from the old washrooms, a very disappointing thing happened. Within two weeks, the clients had written graffiti and all but desecrated the new washrooms. Mr. Bain and the other administrators were shocked. The staff and the clients were not shocked, however. It is exactly what was expected. This was not their home. They were not invested in it. This represented an establishment facility. And their mindset was that they were lashing out at authority and society.

Rick, Mitch, and Debbie had many good times being on the desk from 3:00 to 11:00. Rick was a union rep and a case manager who worked part time, 2:00 to 6:00 and so it provided back up for the desk and also they could discuss union business. About this time, there was a certain client in the house whose name was Pedro Perana. On one of those few nights when Rick was not on the alternate shift, it was a woman named Lena. Lena and Mitch had a good rapport. She was an older single mother and when it was quiet at the desk, oftentimes if it wasn't their break, they would take a cigarette break anyway. They rushed them, of course. They would walk out back, have a cigarette and talk a little, and then come back to make sure things were okay on the desk. While on one of these absences from the desk—the total time was four minutes—this client Pedro was at the window of the office bubble waiting for toiletries and supplies and no attendant was, of course, available. The setup at the front desk at that time had a very small window, which you could hand tickets to the clients through or exchange money or toiletries. All the rest of the office was glassed in like a bubble except for this small little hole like you would see at a cashier's window at the theater.

While Lena and Mitch were gone for their cigarette break, Pedro noticed that the cash register was not too far from this little hole. It was big enough for him to fit his hand through and his arm up to the elbow and he began playing with the buttons of the cash register. Within a very short time, he hit on the right button and the cash register popped open. He simply took the drawer of the cash register out and helped himself to the roles of change and bills that he could get his hands on. Then he neatly put the drawer back into the cash register and closed it. He ran out the door of the building and disappeared.

Within a fraction of the second, as he had run out, Lena and Mitch returned from their cigarette break. When they went back into the building, Mitch went into the front desk area. When Mitch opened the cash register, he got the shock of his life. This was around 10:00 p.m., which was usually the time that Mitch did his accounting for the night and figured out what meal tickets he'd sold, what donations had come in and if the change was accounted for properly. When there was no money in the cash register, Mitch realized what must have happened and checked the surveillance camera and brought it back far enough to see what Pedro Perana had done. Pedro was probably not aware that there was a camera at the front desk.

Mitch panicked and felt very stupid at not having been where he should have been and that such a thing could happen, that someone would rob a charitable organization. Mitch knew that there was only about $50 in the till that day, so he had thought of replacing it himself and not saying anything to anyone. Instead, he decided to call Rick. Rick had a good rapport with Mr. Watson and Rick offered to call Mr. Watson and explain the situation.

Unbelievably, Mr. Watson understood. He knew that the rules allowed for employees to go for breaks sometimes when it was busy. They were allowed to go to the washroom or a smoke for a short time as long as they were not away from the desk for too long and they made sure the area was secure, that the doors had all been locked and the video camera was on before they left. Mitch believed that it was only because of Rick that Mr. Watson was so understanding. When they both came in to work to see Mitch, it was Mitch that they comforted, and then later that window was sealed up so that issue could never happen again.

There were plenty of other access places to hand out tickets or exchange money. At that point, Mr. Watson had Mitch's respect. It was unbelievable that he would stand up like that for Mitch in spite of what the administration might say. Whether it was calculating or not was a question that could only be answered later but for the time being, it was a magnanimous gesture. Mitch would not be disciplined. Of course, that incident eventually changed policy on breaks of any kind without relief at the desk. Pedro Perana happened to be on probation for theft already. Police were called, of course, and an investigation was done. Mitch's name was used, so he was afraid he'd have to go to court as a witness. It was yet another fun part of this job. Fortunately, Pedro confessed in face of the videotape and ended up with thirty days. Unbelievably, he came back to try to check in to the center but Mr. Watson had put a barred for life or restricted service on him not just for the local Redemption Center but for every Redemption Center around the country.

Chapter Three

About this time, there was a memorial service for Ralph Little, who had died on the shift that Debbie and Mitch were on. Mitch was asked to play his music at the event. He did play some church music from time to time. He wrote his own Christian music and had played at some churches and festivals and had even done some recording. So Mitch did his rendition of "I Shall Be Released" by the Band, just himself, and his 12-string and it seemed to go over well. That was the first client Debbie and Mitch had lost since they worked together and it was more traumatic for Debbie than for Mitch. It wasn't that Mitch didn't feel some remorse for the gentleman, it was just that he had seen too much of it, and to give in to those feelings was to become vulnerable. Also about this time, because of pressure from the city, barring and service restriction rules were being revised. Not that there was not already a lot of leniency toward the clients when it came to drinking, addictions, breaking curfew, and abusing staff. Even violence within the facility was now treated with more leniency. The police, the provincial office, and the other shelters and services were overrun with homeless.

Someone had to take responsibility and it was usually the Redemption Center that wound up doing it. If they were to stay in business, they had to take care of these people no matter what their particular issues were, even mental health issues. This was the mandate from the city and the agency. And it had to be done with the same amount of staff and under the worst possible conditions, mostly being totally at the mercy of the client.

Well, as anyone would reasonably expect, this was a recipe for disaster. It started with three particular clients, one after another, all on successive days and it became a chain reaction that brought everybody to the negotiating table including all the union people, Debbie, Mitch, the national rep Trudy, Rick, Mr. Bain, and Mr. Watson. In the end, it was decided that the solution was not so simple.

The first client that they dealt with was a client named Jonathan Mann with a serious mental health issue and an addiction problem. Jonathan was already booked into the center and he was displaying some bizarre behavior. He would stay on the house phone (that was right near the front desk) for hours. He would get insulting with whoever he was talking with on the phone and would swear at the top of his lungs and smash the phone repeatedly against the wall. His behavior began to become quite alarming. He was supposed to be on some psychotropic medication (which he had not been taking) and the word was that he was smoking crack and drinking, also. There was also another issue. He carried a metal briefcase around with him. It was an expensive looking metal briefcase, not the kind you see every day.

When Debbie tried to address his anger issues and his drug use and mixing his illicit drugs with his prescription meds (Lithium, which he was not taking anyway), he became quite indignant, angry, and confrontational. He took his metal briefcase and left it on the front desk outside the bubble and informed us that we had fifteen minutes before the case would explode. Mitch had experienced these kinds of threats from clients before and usually didn't take it very seriously. What homeless person would have the technology besides the ambition to create a bomb and for what purpose? Homeless folks usually did things with an objective in mind like money, bus tickets, or special privileges. What would Jonathan possibly accomplish by blowing up the Redemption Center? After he left the case at the desk, he left the Redemption Center. To take every precaution, which was the mandate, they called police. Several police officers showed up along with the bomb expert. After much discussion and reports that had to be submitted plus police reports, the bomb expert finally felt the case, lifted it, examined it carefully, and then opened it. The thing that made this a little more serious than a regular bomb threat was the case itself because it looked expensive.

Mitch was an encyclopedia of the homeless in Test City and cops and staff from other shelters often phoned him to get his take on a client or to see if he knew their whereabouts. Mitch usually knew if a client's threats were real or not. So then confidently, with four police around him, the expert opened the case. It was empty except for some foam packed inside. The case was taken to be disposed of. Police then went on a hunt for Mann and found him hiding in the bushes a few blocks away. They questioned him on his actions but amazingly did not arrest him, mostly because of his mental health issue. Police left and Jonathan returned to the center within an hour wanting access and a police officer that accompanied him asked us why we would not take him in. We explained the bomb threat and told him that he was service restricted. The administration reviewed the situation and allowed Jonathan back into the center within 48 hours. All the staff threw up their hands in frustration and questioned what possible thought pattern might have brought the administration to this conclusion.

The next day, it was the story of Leslie Warden, another person with a serious mental health issue. Just a young person, about 23 years old, but on psychotropic meds (Clonazapam, a strong dose), he was about as bizarre as you get. He followed none of the rules. Laundry closed at 11:00 p.m. This rule had to be enforced because the machines would keep people awake in the dorm next door. Leslie insisted on starting his laundry at 11:00, the rare time he showed for 11:00 curfew or bed check. He always complained that the snack or the dinner was substandard. He was confrontational and very disrespectful to the women case managers as well as the males. There came a night when he had gone too far, when he came in at 12:30 a.m. assisted by police, stoned out of his mind, as he had been often, and he was refused entry. The police gave Mitch and Debbie a hard time in that they said, "What is this facility for if it's not for people like this?" Mitch ended by explaining, "This is a homeless facility, not a detox, or a mental health facility. This person needs special care." Mitch explained that beside the addictions, mental health issues, and verbal abuse, Leslie had tried to take his life three times. This could be serious or simply a cry for help but they had to enforce the service restriction for tonight.

If they did give Leslie access tonight, it was obvious he would try to commit suicide again, which meant ambulances, police, reports, and then calling police again at 3:00 a.m. (not to mention the trauma if he succeeded). If he did not threaten suicide, he wouldn't sleep anyway. As he was leaving with the policeman, he was swearing at Debbie and Mitch and they were told later that eventually, Leslie went to the city office to complain that he was not given fair treatment. The service restriction stuck and it was for a week. While Mitch and Debbie were off for the weekend, though, a new worker booked him back in the very next day.

The next case was a fellow from Newfoundland by the name of Will Heffernan. He was a chronic alcoholic and a crack user. Every time he was allowed into the center, he promised to do better but he never did. He would drink all the time up in his dorm or the washroom and sneak joints. He would go to the hotel and get drunk and show up at 3:00 a.m. at the front desk stoned out of his mind. Debbie was the kind of person who wanted to try to help these people to the best of her ability. It seemed like everyone she tried to help, however, disappointed her in the end, and crashed. Heffernan was no different.

On another particular night about 10:00 p.m., Heffernan showed up at the front desk stoned out of his mind and Debbie and Mitch had to ask him to leave. The effort of trying to talk to him, however, had been to get him to the point that he might consider detox; he refused. He would not listen to Debbie at all. Many of these guys had a deep-seeded resentment of women, either through divorce or broken family relationships, and they would many times not listen to a woman. Heffernan eventually did go to detox, but the center would not accept him back until he had gone through a seven-day program. Instead, he showed up two days later stoned out of his mind. He had jumped ship on detox. Since Mitch and Debbie were on shift, he was refused re-entry. The thirty-day barring that was put in place (to be reviewed by administration) was again simply pooh-poohed by administration and Heffernan was allowed back into the facility two nights later. He did the same thing again. He slept through Mitch and Debbie's shift but at 3:00 a.m. on Gus's shift, he acted up and had to be removed.

There was a person with a mental health issue who was probably worse than all the rest. His name was Michael Wambanga and he had been wandering the street for at least six months when he came to the center. He had been through some mental health treatment though he refused to take his meds and he had also done some jail time. He was in extremely good shape physically, muscular, chiseled, about 250 pounds and as strong as a tank. He was a black male approximately 24 years old. He had not had a nice time of it, particularly at home, though only some of the details were known. One thing was for sure: He did not like white people. When Mitch went to book him into the shelter, it was obvious that he was unresponsive. Mitch couldn't even get the basic answers out of him—proper spelling of name, sin card, health card, place of origin, citizenship. He was very confrontational and it was glaringly obvious that he had a chip on a shoulder three feet long. Mitch took some time with him to explain the rules but he would not look Mitch in the eye and it was clear that he was not comprehending or accepting the rules as laid out.

With Mitch's view at the front desk of the video monitoring of the TV room, Mitch could see that Michael had settled in and placed his stuff on his bunk and that he was in the TV room. It appeared through the camera, however, as if he was in front of the TV blocking it for anyone to see and dancing to some music that he had put on TV. Mitch could see a lot of animated gestures and postures from the other guys sitting in the TV room. Some had risen to their feet and were waving their hands. At that point, Mitch felt it was time to go down to the TV room. Michael had commandeered the TV and was listening to a dance channel and while he danced, he had his pants down to about his knees, supposedly the style. He was becoming more extreme and he was yelling and going at it with the other clients. When Mitch entered the room, Michael took the TV remote apart and threw the battery cap in one place in the room and the batteries in another place and then broke the remote itself in half and threw those two pieces to different spots in the TV room. Michael then brushed past Mitch and went to his bunk. Mitch had to ask Michael to leave the facility and Michael was very belligerent when Mitch threatened to call police. Michael picked up his stuff from his bunk and left the facility.

Michael never tried to re-enter the center but Mitch saw him many times on the street, freezing on the sidewalk with his pants half down and in a short-sleeve shirt in November in very cold weather or wandering the street harassing people. Police were called many times but Michael was never held in custody or even brought to the emergency psychiatric for assessment. This was a clear case of different agencies within the system not doing their job. So the constant reply was a request to take this person and others like him into the Redemption Center. He's homeless, why can't you care for him? It was a sad state of affairs and even the mental health outreach team, which was supposed to care for the state of these people and make decisions on their placement, simply talked to him several times and released him. Their statement was that he was not a danger to himself or others, which he had been. He was aggressive with other clients and staff, he punched the other clients, kicked the other clients, and kicked cars. Mitch could not believe that he still could not be held, assessed, and helped. After many months of watching Michael go back and forth on the street, the tragedy of it began to occur to Mitch. Although Michael was not a person that Mitch had the training to handle, it did not stop him from feeling sorry for Michael. He tried to get authorities to help and finally it was said that Michael was put under psychiatric assessment, given meds, and was then well-behaved enough to go back and live with his parents. All things considered, however, it probably took a year and two months to get Michael assessed and cared for. Michael was one of the lucky ones, though. He lived and didn't die of exposure or fall into the wrong hands or get into the wrong situation, like getting beaten up on the street or getting arrested and thrown in jail instead of a mental health facility. Thank God, Michael was not one of these tragedies. Mitch had seen enough of those.

Chapter Four

At this point in time, there was a lot of talk from the administration that the staff was being too hard on the clients. All the events that happened in the recent past, all the client incidents, attacks, violence, vandalism, drug use, police calls—still, the administration thought that the staff must be responsible, not their policies. There were two binders full of incident reports that stated differently; still, the administration stuck to its guns that staff were being too tough on the clients when they were service restricted in response to these actions.

During this time, there was a particularly difficult client by the name of Mauro Escobar. This client was impossible. He was always drunk and disorderly on property and demanding about what he wanted, whether it be toiletries, special bed assignments, or the ability to come in late without permission, and he liked the attention of female caseworkers. He was flirtatious, although at this point not to a disciplinary degree.

When this had gone as far as it could and with the new barring policy from the administration, Mitch had the idea of putting this issue before Mr. Watson, being that it was a specialized issue and none of the staff seemed able to deal with this person. Mr. Watson accepted the challenge. Mauro was called into the office in the middle of the day and confronted with the fact that he had been drinking and disorderly in the house, which was not compliant with the rules, besides the fact that some of his comments to staff were inappropriate. He showed up to the interview drunk and probably stoned on something else. Mr. Watson did his client-centered empathy thing with Mauro. Mr. Watson had no intention of barring him or service restricting him. He simply wanted Mauro to agree to comply somewhat with the rules of the house, especially being that he was getting free room and board out of the deal. Mauro had not even contributed any of his disability check toward his stay. Mauro's reaction was not receptive. Mr. Watson said, "Mauro, you have to change the way you do things if you're going stay here. We would really like to help you and we're trying to cooperate with your situation but you will have to be a little more compliant than you have been."

Well, Mauro's reaction was, "This is none of your fucking business. You're supposed to give me a place to stay. You people are supposed to do that shit the government tells you to do. This is charity and you're supposed to help me. This is my home; I have no place else to stay."

Mr. Watson kept up the client-centered empathy thing. "We're very sorry you feel that way, Mr. Escobar, but there are other clients to consider. There have been some fights and arguments because of your behavior and staff are also limited as to what they can do for you."

Mauro's reply was, "This is none of your fucking business. I'll do what I fucking want to do and there's nothing you can do about it." At this point, Mr. Watson stood up to move past Mauro and leave the office.

Mauro picked up a pair of scissors that was lying on the desk and reached over and grabbed Mr. Watson and put the scissors against his throat and said, "If you don't let me stay here and mind your own business, I'm going to kill you." Mr. Watson stepped back and asked Mauro to calm down and phoned the front desk to ask for assistance. Big Don phoned 911 and showed up at Mr. Watson's office to escort Mauro from the building. As soon as he saw Don, he left without incident. Mr. Watson barred Mauro for six months.

Another incident in which Mr. Bain was referred to with the F word, the client was given a year. At a later union-management meeting, Mitch raised the question, "Why is it okay when administration are threatened to bar someone for a year or life but not when staff are threatened a couple times a week?" Mitch's statement was, "Do you understand now what we're talking about that it's not all about the empathy? There are some of the unfortunates that fall through the cracks but there is the criminal element and mental health issues also and security has to be a priority." It was pooh-poohed as a one-time incident and the administration refused to discuss the issue as usual. Health and Safety called the Labor Board to come and examine the situation and the incident report but there was not a representative from Health and Safety or many others around. Mr. Watson was very persuasive and explained to them that it was a one-time incident and there was not violence on a regular basis. They accepted his explanation and did not return.

Still on some level, the administration finally realized that this was a serious situation they were dealing with. It was not just caring for the homeless. It was a security situation. Add to that the fact that the third floor of our building was designated for Federal parolees and when the some of the Federal parolees came off parole and had nowhere to stay, they would stay in the shelter, which added yet another criminal element.

Back to the story of Mauro. He was arrested but not charged for his threat of Mr. Watson. He was back drunk and wreaking havoc by the next day. The union and the staff threw up their arms at these latest developments. It seemed no point talking to the administration; their only focus was going to be filling the beds at any cost and if someone was going to be a casualty, it would be a front desk person, not the administration. So the client-centered stupidity continued until it reached a fever pitch and the casualties numbered in the dozens and across the field as previously stated in the hundreds. Workers were chewed up and spit out and no one seemed to shed a tear about it.

This affair that was supposedly going on between Blain the client and Stacey the program director continued on even though it had proved a scandal, even though it was yet unverified. Now there were rumors, some true, some not, about different clients and different staff or staff or clients from probation on the third floor and staff in the other shelters. It was becoming a very confusing place to work. One night, in fact, when Mitch was out in the back having a cigarette, from a distance, he observed a quite attractive, well-dressed blond being allowed in through a back door. By the time Mitch got over there to investigate, they were gone but Mitch reported this to the third floor. That night, there was a shakedown and search in case one of the probationary people was sneaking this girl in.

In the end, it was discovered that it was a staff person who was sneaking hookers in at night, though it was never proved. It was still suspected that Eva was having an affair with at least one client. And that she was meeting clients in bars as was Stacey and their friend, the coordinator of the hospital release program, Katie T. Mitch had witnessed the administration's reaction to and response to some of these situations in the past, not just the administration of the Redemption Center, but the administration of all these types of operations: denial first, then some interest, then perhaps an investigation and usually resulting in no action at all. These organizations and their procedures really made Mitch laugh sometimes.

When the local administration would not investigate, the city would step in to investigate gossiping, not keeping confidentiality until the situation became blown way out of proportion until the time they had their kangaroo court meeting in which they usually had no proof. The accused would deny it and it would be over. And the word would travel all over the place that Eva was being investigated or Stacey was being investigated or someone on the front desk was being investigated for selling cigarettes or some such nonsense.

The administration usually didn't involve police because these were usually not legal matters but policy matters and they had no investigative right or experience. Many times, it was a harmless workplace romance that needed to be dealt with but they acted as if they were investigating a murder case. An officer from the third floor, a detective in fact, once commented to Mitch that these administration people should be investigated. They were not police or detectives or investigators. If they thought there were grounds to suspect someone of crossing the boundaries, having an affair with a client, stealing, or selling contraband out of the center, they had the perfect right to fire them. However, in most of these cases, criminal liability was not an issue and many of them should never have been investigated.

Also, their investigative practices resembled the KGB or the Gestapo rather than a charitable organization trying to reach out to someone in trouble or help provide answers.

Eva was seen in restaurants with a client drinking beer and a message was retrieved from her office phone from that client. The message seemed very familiar, as if they were friends not client/worker. Specific dates, times, and issues were mentioned. Finally, Eva was called into the office and Rick was the person that she chose to defend her as union rep. After many questions and Eva's denial, she was let off. She claimed nothing had happened but from that point on, she began taking a lot of time off.

Rita on the desk was also very ill as well as stressed out and she began to take a lot of time off. She was a desk person who was also implicated with a client but it was obvious that she was innocent. Unfortunately, she went through a long period of harassment by that client. The client definitely had a fatal attraction for her, which caused him to phone her address and show up at her house drunk, harassing her husband and kids. The whole thing was insulting to Rita and her family and the agency took no part in helping with the situation. Further, they kept allowing this person, Ritchie, back into the facility. Besides the fact that this gentleman was continually getting into fights with other people in the shelter, he would come in drunk and start brawls. He had been barred countless times and let off the hook. But he made this allegation to Mr. Watson about Rita and him having a mutual affair. Mr. Watson called her in and Mitch was her representative. She denied it all yet nothing was done to this client who continued to wreak havoc in the shelter, on the food line, and in her personal life. The longest time out he was given was three months and was allowed back into the facility again.

This kind of logic neither Mitch nor the desk staff nor the caseworkers nor many other clients or the union itself could completely understand. The national union rep (a middle-aged, militant union person) who was in for a visit during the client management meeting, walked in as clients were coming and going through the front door that was supposed to be a security door. During the meeting, Mr. Watson and Mr. Bain bragged about the security measures that they had put in place in the center. Trudy had to laugh and commented that she walked right in through the front door and had not been noticed. How good could this security system be? Mr. Bain and Mr. Watson were speechless at the comment.

The administration's idea of security was always cameras. There was a camera for every access, all interior hallways, and every part of the building except for private rooms, dorms, and bathrooms. Entrances and the exterior part of the building were covered also, including a panoramic view of the front and of the back parking lot. The problem was that there was only one staff on duty most of the time—one on the desk and the caseworker up in the case management office. The front desk was busy and many times the caseworker had many clients to see. You couldn't watch the camera constantly and someone could be in imminent danger by time you did see anything. Even with panic buttons, if the front desk person did run up to help the caseworker, he was not a security person. What was he supposed to do? Get in a fight with the clients in order to regain order? He couldn't leave the caseworker helpless in a desperate situation while waiting for the police. Security was what was needed and it had already been started at other shelters in other cities and, as previously mentioned, at the provincial branch of the welfare office. There was plenty of security there, that's for sure. There were several workers on duty at the same time including several males plus the security guards. Of course, this was not the kind of image that the Redemption Center wanted to show. These agencies didn't want to advertise that stuff; they wanted to portray the warm and fuzzy stuff. They want to show a welcoming and open environment. It didn't matter how much mayhem transpired as long as they could give the image of being an openly charitable organization.

A security guard, or a few security guards, was definitely what was needed but Mitch was sure that it would not happen until someone got hurt. The last time someone got hurt, it was Trina who was trying to get the guys out of the TV room in the morning so the cleaners could start cleaning. They were sleeping all over the furniture and wouldn't move. She got them all out except for one whose name was Brad who was a very big fellow—6-foot-4, 325 pounds. When she tried to give him an ultimatum that he would have to leave or be service restricted, he threw his gym bag at her, which was a very heavy bag, and knocked her down.

She wasn't seriously injured but it started the whole case that the two night men would have to stay late in the morning in order to wake the guys up and get them out of the TV room before they left to go home so that the female caseworkers would not have to deal with this type of situation. The desk person, usually a male, then became the desk person, the financial person, and now the bouncer and the person who had to do the paperwork for all those who were signed in and designated for the night, not to mention the end-of-the-month accounting. It was a lot to ask for the money that was being paid. There was many a time when Mitch was on the desk trying to do the food line, selling tickets, punching tickets, making change, and dealing with whatever scuffles might be on the food line itself when he would be called down to the kitchen because there was a fight in the kitchen or the dining room. So then, Mitch would have to hold the food line up to run downstairs to break up a fight, calling police before he left. He would have to do an incident report when he returned, while the food line was irate that they were late for dinner.

When these complaints came up at the union-management meeting, more cameras were put in and it was decided that there would be a crossover afternoon person, an extra person to work 4:00 p.m. to 9:00 p.m. These were the very busy supper time/book in hours. Rick, who was already a part-timer in discharge (and the other union guy), got the assignment and Debbie, Rick, and Mitch worked well together and had some laughs for the short time this position lasted.

News soon came out, though, that the hospital release program would eventually be closed, and those people (which included Eva and Katie T.) would be out of a job. Administration's problem was solved, and they never spoke of the incidences with the two of them or that they were being investigated again. They added a few more cameras, the crossover person that worked 5 hours, and that was about all that changed. The police had their own beefs with the system, however, and made it known. They could be at the Redemption Center five times a day, not counting the ambulances, fire trucks, or EMS. Eventually, police met with Redemption Center administrators and told them that they should have their own security police because they could not be there as often or as quickly as required, considering the number of situations that went on at the Redemption Center.

Chapter Five

The staff casualties became so real and so huge, it made it hard to work in that environment anymore. It seemed that anyone who Mitch had ever really cared about in the workplace was now gone. There were a lot of younger people and people who really didn't want Mitch's input or any input from more experienced workers. Their thought was that their school curriculum was the answer as to how to be a successful caseworker or frontline worker. This, of course, was not the case. It was nice to have a good mixture of both the educational and the practical, but one without the other in either case was, from a worker's standpoint, dangerous. At least the experienced workers knew what they were dealing with. Younger workers were all full of vim and vigor but without any practical knowledge as to how to impart the ideals that they wanted to affect the client with. To them it was all about addiction rehab and adherence to rules, which without the ideal was just rote.

Further, their excessive catering and empathy toward the clients led to an atmosphere of enablement. Many of them were in effect enablers and counterproductive. It became quite a trial for Mitch to go to work during those days. His afternoon shift was the busiest shift. He never knew what he would find when he came in. There could be a fight in progress or someone who needed an ambulance or a mix up with the tickets or the cash. Administration didn't really care about two staff fighting, and there was a lot of that, as long as business continued as usual. It was one thing after the other and by time the night was over, it was usually several things. You really didn't even know if you were going home after your shift because many times the relief person would phone in sick and it was hard to find anyone else to cover the front desk in a pinch. People simply wouldn't answer their phones if they saw the call display said Redemption Center. Mitch got to the point where one shift was plenty and after a week of shifts, he could be a babbling basket case.

Gus quit one day after eleven years of service. He resigned because the administration wouldn't give him his vacation when they couldn't get relief for him. It was the last straw for him. He quit and became a tow truck driver. Talking to him a few weeks later, he said that it was the best thing he ever did. "The lack of stress is a daily tonic." Meanwhile, the Redemption Center, wanting to improve their facility, applied for some government grants and got them. They decided to build a new fire escape on the back of the building because the building was built in 1958. They could have repaired the old one. It was in much better shape than many of the fire escapes in older buildings around town. They could have done this for fractional cost but instead, they decided to build a brand new fire escape. While codes have changed, both the city and the construction companies saw them coming. The final price tag on this fire escape was over $300,000. The fire escape looked like a state of the art steel stairway up to a landing pad. There were only three floors in the Redemption Center but each one had an elaborate landing and stairways going to every door. It was the joke of the city and the word was that the fire escape was worth more than the building and would be there long after the building was gone. The same kind of joking went on about the washrooms.

They got a grant to renovate the washrooms that went over budget because it was found that there was asbestos in the washrooms that had to be removed. Where did they find the money for these over-budget projects? Further, where did all the money go when it didn't get spent on projects? For example, many times the caseworker staff would not show up for work. These caseworkers belonged to a certain program that was funded from outside the agency by a government program. When the caseworker was absent and not replaced (which the administration did often), clients were not being serviced and there should have been no funding for that day. Still, most of the time these absences were not reported and the Redemption

Center continued to collect the money. Private rooms were also being renovated and made more up to date for the clients, which also went over budget that somehow the Redemption Center swallowed.

When it came to health and safety issues though, or making things more safe for the clients and staff, there was never enough money. At contract time, also, the Redemption Center was apparently broke. They showed all their financial sheets and reports showing that people did not get raises, including their hierarchy or their officers.

Around this time, the New Apostles Shelter was also involved in a project federally and provincially funded but that had gone way over budget. This was to be a homeless center showplace. It was to include two subsidized housing buildings—co-ed—a clothing facility to provide free clothing for the homeless, and a state of the art kitchen with the former chef from one of the biggest hotels in the city. It was also to include a mental health task force and administration offices for all the execs from directors to managers of this organization. This new state-of-the-art center was also to provide women services in all aspects and a drop-in center for the homeless.

The local neighborhood fought this project for five years through the courts and local political system and eventually lost. The legal battle to gain the right to build The New Apostles Center, which would be the biggest homeless center in the city was $1,000,000 in legal fees for this agency. A $25,000,000 to $35,000,000 estimate for this homeless showplace grew to be $50,000,000 by time it was finished. The administration of this agency then asked the employees to contribute 3 percent of their paychecks to see the project completed. Mitch's friend Lou Ann was now a union steward in that organization, and of course the answer from the union was a flat no.

The public rationale was that if this organization had $50,000,000 to spend, why didn't they just take over one of the many derelict old buildings or abandoned buildings in the city and increase payments to the poor, help them more with food, clothing, and accommodation instead of building a Taj Mahal for the homeless that would administrate everything as usual and provide little by the time all the red tape was done.

Mitch had worked for this organization before and knew what it was like. Not only did they have the caseworkers mopping floors, cleaning toilets, cooking meals, and breaking up fights, they had them doing all the regular work a caseworker does. When they had the nerve to call you a caseworker, it was rather insulting. They were always moralistic and judgmental and expected everyone who worked for them to have the same moral ideals and judgment they did. They wanted you to be part of the place in that they wanted you to work until you dropped, and they wanted your financial contributions, but when it came to decision-making, the employee had no say.

There were some very good reasons why working, tax-paying citizens didn't want this kind of thing in their neighborhood. One of the other homeless shelters in the city that was basically a drop in, called the Beasley Center, had ruined the neighborhood that they were in. Residents walking their dogs would find needles. People would be accosted for donations or handouts while walking down the street. Sometimes if they refused, there would be threats or violence. Those who were too drunk and disorderly or under the influence to enter the shelter, many times, slept out in the neighborhood on the grass across the street or on someone's lawn. The cost to the others in that neighborhood was not considered when Beasley Center was suggested or built. There should be help for the homeless and addicted and those with mental health issues—help for those people who have legitimately fallen through the cracks in our society. It had to be done in a way that was fair to everyone, however. And as previously mentioned, every agency had to take its part.

This was never the case and that's why Test City became homeless central. That's why all the other communities who didn't want the homeless in their community shipped them to homeless central. That's also why the grant money kept coming in and Test City always received the maximum in support for social services. But it was also turning Test City into a garbage dump. Not only every agency had to take responsibility for the homeless but every community had to take responsibility for their own homeless, also.

Mitch saw so many good people go down or leave the system because the system didn't work. Mitch's former partner, Julie, left to become a police officer, however she knew quite well before she left that she could never stay in the business she was in. She knew very well, also, what the issues were. If the administrations of these organizations and agencies ever denied any of the above information, there were legions of staff and clients who would come forward and state their case. Although Julie was one of the people that you could count on to stick it out and she left with a clean slate, many others that left like Gus, quit because they couldn't take it anymore.

There was Cindy, who was formerly Mitch's union partner and steward for two years, who left with five years service. There was Trina Gonzales, who was the coordinator before Katie T. There was Annette, who simply couldn't handle the stress anymore at sixty-five years old. There was Rita, who had to go on leave of absence because she had a nervous breakdown. There was Don, who went off because of a heart problem. There was Edith, who was Mitch's first boss when he came into the organization. She was fired for being too hard on the staff and having a promiscuity issue with a resident construction worker. The program director previous to her was Mr. Rector, who was fired because some of the disgruntled nurses claimed that he said some inappropriate things to women staff. It was later proved that he said nothing that could have been construed as suggestive but it was too late. His reputation was ruined and he left in disgrace, as would Virginia (caseworker) who had to go off because the stress of the job was complicating her pregnancy. Many others as well as these left over the years, most hurt and disillusioned.

The incidents that hurt the most were the ones that happened when Mitch was still at the Jesus Saves Kitchen. All of those that he had come up with and who helped him learn the ropes were all disposed of, one by one. Doug Waters was one of those who would pay the huge price for wanting to help. He was one of those who had worked his way up from being an alcoholic, a drug addict, and a dealer, to becoming a worker who was clean and sober. He had a pain issue, though, and he eventually had to have two plastic knees put in. He was in so much pain, sometimes, it was unbearable but he dealt with it and rarely complained. Sometimes he had to take pain pills, though. And sometimes, he took too many pain pills. During a meeting one day, while everyone was standing around listening to a speech by the executive director, Doug's knees gave out and he collapsed. When those around—Mitch included—tried to help him, it was obvious that he had too many pain pills in him because he was speaking incoherently. The next day, he was no longer working at the Jesus Saves Kitchen. He was terminated without cause. This was the empathy that a worker of six years received.

The next casualty was a volunteer of German descent named Helmut, a one-time kitchen worker. He did a very good job. He worked harder, in fact, than most paid staff. He had a habit of speaking his mind, however, and at one point he was trying to set some boundaries down with the clients. His was trying to tell them how many helpings of dinner were reasonable because some would take three, four, or five helpings and leave no food for anyone else. The clients rebelled, of course, which led to a meeting with Director Bob.

Executive Director Bob told him he was being too harsh with clients and stated to him, "You work for me and you will do what I say." Helmut's response was, "I work for God, not for you, and anytime that you feel that I'm not doing a good enough job, just tell me so." Helmut also became a casualty the next day.

These flashbacks helped Mitch work out and understand what was now going on at the Redemption Center. Staff was disposable at all these agencies. The last straw, however, was probably Michael Lang. Here was a fellow who had worked his way up through the ranks, rehabbed, and was a 10-year employee of Jesus Saves Kitchen. He developed the disease leukemia during his last days there. He wanted reduced hours but they kept calling him in for extra shifts all the time because the problem was the same at the Jesus Saves Kitchen as with all these other agencies. Absenteeism ran rampant. About this time, they brought in a hatchet person called Katie Farrell, who was very particular about running the complete show herself, from the dollars and cents portion to the scheduling and client case management portion. No one had access to anything except her and all calls and clients were funneled through her. This gave the illusion of making her look like she was important, as clients, staff, and other agencies were always phoning asking for her because when she had become program director that's the way she designed it. However, she was rarely there to answer the calls or see the clients or take care of the details. The month-end financial was always at least a month late and usually incorrect. She was fired from a previous job for tinkering with the numbers and the same kind of controlling behavior.

Most people didn't want to work under Katie, and about that time, Mike insisted he could do no more shifts. He went off on disability. Mitch looked after Mike for awhile. He looked after his cat, took him back and forth to his appointment, and visited him in the hospital. Other than Mitch and his friendship, Mike basically wanted to be left alone. The Jesus Saves Kitchen held him up as a hero of sorts and totally exploited the fact that he was a colleague and a fantastic employee. They wanted him to come for parties and appearances and the odd shift, but he would not do it. Eventually, he died alone in his apartment. When Mike had not contacted Bob or Mitch, Bob, the director, got the superintendent to allow him in to Mike's apartment and called police. It was months before his estate was settled because none of his relatives would show up to claim him or even his money. Mike was like a mentor to Mitch. He taught him the softer side of dealing with clients through his patience and rationalizing with them.

Mitch learned a lot about the Jesus Saves Kitchen itself, also, although Mitch already knew a lot about clients and had similar ideas about boundaries, empathy, and how education and experience joined to make a successful worker. When Mike died and Katie took over full-time service as program director, Mitch resigned his manager's job and just took a job on front desk, part-time nights, three days a week. After Mike died, though, and all the things that happened, it was time for Mitch to move on to the Redemption Center. He always carried a piece of Mike with him from then on and sang a song at Mike's memorial that left not a dry eye in the house. It also made him twice as staunch an advocate for the rights of workers and how many of them fell through the cracks, just like the clients. In fact, more than a few had become clients again because of the brutality of this work environment and the system itself. Mitch hoped that the insanity at the kitchen was a one-off but he quickly learned that the Redemption Center was just as bad, if not worse. They were all the same. Once Mitch was at the Redemption Center for several years, he tried to get his other friend, Nick D (permanent, full-time night person at the Kitchen) into the Redemption Center without much success.

About a year after Julie had left the Redemption Center, Mitch was still in touch with Nick on a regular basis, sometimes on shift because they referred clients back and forth and sometimes at home. Mitch heard the news that Nick might no longer be with the Redemption Center. He had been with them for fifteen years. It was supposedly an argument with a female staff, 21 years old, fresh out of school. A client who was drunk and disorderly was being belligerent to Nick and Nick was responding in kind, laying down boundaries to the client and the client was asked to leave. The other staff, who we will call Marnie, stepped in and said that Nick was being too hard on the client, right in front of the client. The big wigs from the female administration were called in with Lora, the new executive director, and Katie, the PD. They decided that the client was not to be punished and that Nick must write an apology letter to Marnie. Nick would not write an apology to their satisfaction and when he would not comply, he was terminated with cause so that they could withhold severance and termination pay. Hearing and seeing all this from Mitch's new spot at the Redemption Center was hard to fathom and the same thing was happening here even with a union. It was brutal what had become of the Christian ethic that they all got into this business for. It did not even resemble what it once was. Who could fix a mess like this or find any redemption in the work that they were now in?

Chapter Six

It seemed like to Mitch who was a devout Christian (despite his shortcomings) that not only the Christian helping agencies but the Christian church itself had slipped into a sad state of affairs. As far as Mitch was concerned, when Christianity became an organization instead of an organism, it ceased to be effective. If you really believed that the Christian church was a living thing, what happened when it ceased to become the living thing, full of the love, true empathy, and care that it was designed to be? It became an organization whose first priority was business. It was hypocrisy. It was much like the Pharisees in days of Christ. As he put it, "You are like whited sepulchers all fair and clean without but within full of dead men's bones and all corruption." This reminded Mitch also of another scripture from Revelation which most Bible scholars agree is a description of some facets of the church and what it would be like when Christ returned. The Scripture reads, (Rev. 3-15) "I know that you are neither hot or cold. I wish you were either hot or cold, but because you are neither, I will spew you out of my mouth."

As mentioned earlier, it seemed like the bottom line was all that really mattered anymore and Mitch didn't believe that the clients were any more important to the administration than the staff were. They were all incidental. It was a money machine just like any other business. There was much misappropriation of funds, also. An example would be the parking concession that parked cars for all the big events at the arena across the street. The Redemption Center had the only parking lot in the area and they charged $10 a car. It was all cash under the table and none of it was declared. Some went to the organization and the rest was split among those who parked cars. Mitch had rarely even heard Christianity preached within the center. There was a Bible study during the day when all the staff was working and clients were not even allowed in the building, so no one ever showed up. There were some token barbecues for staff and clients. There was the odd event at Christmas time. But the Christian ethic and the Christian message were not preached and barely mentioned within the structure or the framework of the true work of the Redemption Center. In fact, it was almost taboo to be talked about. The addiction model was talked about as well as detox, cognitive skills, how to get your life back on track, find an apartment, and find a job. That was all done through an educational system method of case management referral, casework, and advocacy. Christianity was never mentioned.

The Christian aspect of how to overcome your problems through renewal in Christ and a study of the Scriptures or going to church and becoming part of a good solid Christian group was also never mentioned. Little by little, the message was watered down to the point where the administration didn't bother with it at all.

When Test City demanded more stringent rules and ways of dealing with clients and totally put the responsibility on the shelters, Redemption Center didn't even oppose it or mention their Christian place in the community. The Christian message and mandate was not even considered a factor. They all sold out and not one stood up for their Christian ethics. It was indicative of the problems that went on within the shelters and it was not the way it was originally intended. For example, when Mitch first worked at the Jesus Saves Kitchen, it really was what its name suggested and everyone had respect for it for that reason. The new system was a failure and it made for even more disenfranchised and unhappy clients and staff. Further, the administration did not want people talking about these kinds of things. They were afraid of what the world would think of their agency. That society at large might think that they made an unholy alliance and fed from the public trough until the administrators of that public trough became the bosses and these Christian organizations simply flunkies and lackeys who did what they were told and let their true ethics slide.

As earlier mentioned, around this time there were more and more clients who were needier than ever. Mitch could not handle it anymore. His health was beginning to suffer. He had severe headaches as well as chronic hypertension (blood pressure issues) and an anxiety disorder based on the fact that every time he came to work, it was like the gunfight at the OK Corral. Mitch was getting too old for this kind of work anymore. The issue with Blain and Stacey continued. They were apparently having relations in her office with the door locked and the blinds drawn. They had been seen out together in public drinking and eating and on dates. Eva had taken some time off claiming stress, as well as Katie T. Debbie, as previously mentioned, had now become quite popular with more than a few of the clients and she tried to run events like movies and bingo nights and card nights, even sometimes at her own expense.

The problem with Debbie was that she emotionally invested in clients and as each one fell (as they usually did), they took a piece of her with them until she could not handle it anymore.

PART III: Superstar Social Worker Syndrome

Chapter One

As previously mentioned, Debbie and Stacey continued to bang heads. Debbie had a form of superstar social work syndrome, even though she was naively good hearted. She adopted clients en masse or one by one and tried to make a difference in their lives. Her first try was with a fellow called Richard Arliss. She had a few chats with him and worked with him a lot. Through the shelter, she found him a day job working construction and sent him to detox. At that point, he had supposedly stopped drinking and smoking pot. She had also (against the other caseworker Trina's advice) got him into a private room at the center. Mitch was skeptical from the beginning but Debbie chalked that up to his jadedness.

Meanwhile, Richard was drinking in his room the whole time but every time Debbie caught him, she would berate him and he would repent for a few days and continue again. Technically, according to the rules, he should have been evicted at that point. One of the problems was that Richard was so attracted to Debbie that even when he was drunk, he would show up at the desk and try to talk to her and make conversation. If he had just gone to his room or to bed, he would not have got in so much trouble. She indulged it to a degree and allowed him to continue. Because of this, he became more enabled and braver. He drank in his room more often, smoked pot, and had visitors. Eventually, Mitch had to protest to Debbie (but he didn't tell the administration) because other clients were getting the idea that they could do the same and it was starting a trend around the center.

One night, Richard caused quite a lot of trouble at the center. He had come back late—drunk and stoned—and started to make trouble. He was making a scene at the front desk flirting with Debbie and trying to start fights with other clients. He didn't want to stop talking to Debbie for a minute, so when another client needed something from the desk, he would block their way and interfere. Against Mitch's better judgment, Debbie allowed Richard to go to his room and go to bed—of course he didn't do that.

Instead, he invited other clients into his room and began having a party. At this point, Mitch said to Debbie, "This is enough, I can't cover you anymore if you allow this stuff to continue." Mitch and Debbie went up to Richard's room and asked him to leave. Richard was abusive and threatening toward Debbie and Mitch. Police were called and Richard was removed. He was allowed back into the shelter by administration with Debbie's approval within 48 hours. She did not learn that her continuing empathy was not going to help. Then he betrayed her for the last time by taking his paycheck and disappearing for three days on a drunken bender and was fired from his job in the bargain. At that point, she finally knew that Richard was not going to change, at least not anytime soon. He was evicted from his room at the center and barred for three months. Even though Debbie felt foolish for allowing the situation with Richard to go so far, she was hardheaded and determined to make a success of a client so that she could say her style of casework was successful. Her theory was that being a buddy to the guys and proving to them that you were one of them and not an authority figure would help them to change because they would have someone like them to talk to and relate to but who had their act together. But street life and addictions in particular have no friends.

Debbie's next project was a fellow named Johnny Tupper, and Mitch believed that not only was he attracted to Debbie but also that Debbie had a soft spot for him. He was constantly in fights at the center and though he was not a traditional type drunk (in that he handled his booze well), he loved to fight when he was drunk. He had to be a macho man type. He had been barred from the center many times and Debbie decided to take him on as a client and start advocating for him. They would spend long hours talking up in the casework office.

She did the same as she had done for Richard. She helped find him a job and she stuck up for him when he got in trouble with the administration for fighting, usually justifying it by saying that he was just protecting the peace of the shelter by fighting those who were causing trouble. Whenever Johnny showed up after work, Debbie would drop everything and go and meet with him up in the caseworker's office.

There came a certain night when there was an abusive client named Glenn giving Debbie a very hard time up in the office and started calling her names. He then stormed out of her office and proceeded to talk on the house phone, swearing and screaming at whoever was on the other end of line. He slammed the phone down so hard that he broke it. Johnny happened to be walking in as all this was going on. He decided that he was going to protect Debbie's honor by giving Glenn a beating. Debbie came out of the office and interceded and told Glenn to leave the property. As Glenn came down the stairs and came to the front desk to complain about the situation to Mitch, Debbie and Johnny walked out the front door. As Glenn emerged from the building, Johnny walked up to him and started throwing punches; strangely enough, Debbie was holding Johnny's coat. Glenn was beaten up fairly seriously with a cracked lip and a broken tooth. Police were called but Johnny had left the property. Debbie told the police that Glenn was completely to blame and that Johnny was only defending himself, which was not the case. This is also the information that she related on the incident report. Mitch stayed out of the situation. He told Debbie, however, that what she was doing was wrong and it was the last time that she could advocate for a client when the client was wrong or because she happened to be partial to the client. The client Glenn returned the next day and complained to Mr. Watson.

Mr. Watson reviewed the videotape at the time of the incident and came to the conclusion that Debbie had not only lied on her incident report but had lied to police. Since Mitch was not privy to the situation, his opinion was not asked. Still, Johnny was given yet another chance and he continued to do the same thing over and over again. He wouldn't be in the house for two days when he would get into another fight and thinking that Debbie was his advocate and protector enabled him and allowed him to continue.

The last fight he got into was with Randy, the client from the Jesus Saves Kitchen, who was no stranger to fighting himself. Again, the fight took place right out front of the building. Randy never threw a single punch but sat on the ground with his hands over his head while Johnny continued to pummel him repeatedly and Debbie stood out on the street watching. Police were called but Randy preferred not to lay any charge, considering that he had just been released from jail himself. Again, Mr. Watson and Mr. Bain heard about this the next day. When they reviewed the tape, they finally came to the conclusion that Johnny Tupper must leave and Debbie must get a written warning. He was barred for six months but never did return.

After that incident, Debbie's longtime boyfriend, Don, finally asked her to marry him, out of the blue. Debbie seemed to lose her enthusiasm after she lost a few more clients and began taking a lot of time off. She also had a leg injury that didn't help. Still, she tried to continue running events for the guys like bingo and movie nights and Halloween parties. But really little of it had any effect on the guys. They just began to consider her an easy mark. She had such a lot to deal with herself that she was really in no condition to help anyone else. She was a spendthrift, an *eataholic*, and she couldn't keep 2 cents in her pocket at any time. She was not a bad person (in her heart), though, but she had not had an easy time of it from childhood on and she was just trying to make other people's lives better. She was just trying to give those guys the things that she never had and treat them in a way that she had never been treated. Anyway, at about this point, she began taking a lot of time off work and it was upsetting the administration something awful.

While all this was happening, the saga between Stacey and Blain continued and intensified. Blain was starting to make no secret of their new relationship. Stacey was trying to keep a low profile but Blain was bragging to all his friends how he was having an affair with the Program Director of the Redemption Shelter Center. There were a lot of rumors and questions by the administration but nothing concrete had happened at this juncture to prove that Blain and Stacey were actually having an affair. While all this was happening in the background with Stacey, there was very little support for the staff from her or upper management. She had been taking a lot of time off and with an impending marriage, she had other things on her mind. Her marriage was supposed to be to a famous Canadian artist. The engagement and the stag and doe had already taken place and the impending date was not too far in the future, only about six weeks. Meanwhile, the rumors of the affair with Blain continued.

During all this, there was very little support for Debbie and Mitch and the things they were going through with the changing shelter system. The city had taken over. Pretty well all the rules and regulations had changed and there was no more service restriction to speak of. There were a lot of referrals of different kinds and it was a full house every night. Clients were allowed to stay in house 24/7 and there were fights, disputes, and addictions, and staff were rarely able to discipline clients in any way without first dealing with the administration.

During this time, Debbie and Mitch had an incident with a fellow named John Land. John had booked into the house around snack time about 7:00 p.m. and although he had a few under his belt, he seemed somewhat coherent and Mitch allowed him to go for snack. He became very confrontational with Debbie about what snack was available and wound up giving her an extremely hard time. When she challenged his childish behavior, she was called a fat pig that could only give blowjobs. At that point, Mitch was called at the front desk. He showed down in the dining room immediately and Johnny Tupper, who had mysteriously slipped in for snack even though he was barred from the facility, was already starting to get aggressive with John Land. Mitch asked John to leave but he would not. Johnny Tupper and several others were ready to kill Land. Not to cause a huge melee, Mitch gently grabbed John by the arm and began to lead him out. Mitch had known John for years and although he was still swearing at Debbie and resisting Mitch's coaxing, he began to leave. As they got out the dining room door on the way up the stairs, John began to throw punches. Mitch grabbed him by the hood of his jacket and began to pull him up the stairs as he was swinging punches that were landing behind Mitch because Mitch had him by the hood. Mitch ejected him through the door but not without a warning from John that he would return and kill Debbie. When this information was brought to the administration, John only received a 48-hour service restriction and although he didn't return within the next few weeks, the punishment was extremely lenient. As usual, the administration sided with the client and this taught Debbie that it was about being lenient to the clients and only when they're offended, time and time again, would the administration finally discipline them with any authority, barring them for six months or a year.

Debbie had to try to deal with that in spite of all else that was going on in her life. Because clients can be extremely abusive, swearing at staff, calling them names, and treating them badly, Debbie tried to be lenient, but whenever she tried to discipline a client, the administration would usually reverse it. There was a third client she had a real affinity for and his name was Mike Smit. She found a job for him and tried to integrate him into the community and got him a private room at that Redemption Center. Eventually, she helped him save enough money for an apartment and got him on the list for subsidized housing. He seemed to have cleaned up and was going to detox. He was a regular member at AA meetings and to all outward appearances, it seemed that he had totally changed. This was a Debbie success story—the client that she nurtured had actually made it. The problem is that all you know, as a worker, is the person that you see in front of you for the limited time that you see them. You don't know what's going on behind closed doors or in people's minds; even psychiatrists have a hard time with that.

Mike was carrying some pain from childhood—pain of abuse and neglect and of a failed marriage—and he was not really doing as well as he said he was. He told Debbie he was doing well so as not to alarm her because he cared about her, however he was not doing well. He was taking a lot of antidepressant and sleep medication, some of which he was prescribed and some which was not, and he was drinking a lot. One night, he had a few too many and a few too many pills; he overdosed and died. Debbie was a basket case when she found out the news and when she told Mitch, he was somewhat shocked himself, though he didn't think that Mike was actually towing the line as he had told Debbie. When he died, it was about the last straw for Debbie. She could not be there anymore even though she made the pretense for a while.

At about this time, the whole shelter system was changing to residence programs, moving clients from shelters to off-site housing with worker support. It was a big success on paper and was taking many people out of the shelter system. In reality, however, the clients were doing no better and it was actually just an excuse to eventually close down the shelters and remove the safety net as they had done with the mental health act. As well, the city now had total control to dictate how each individual distributor of services was to administrate the shelter system. They even wanted to dictate which office the caseworkers would work out of and what format they would work under. There were to be no more caseworkers in the shelters. Just one token caseworker during the day to deal with whatever problems might occur. They didn't take into consideration all the things that a caseworker did. A caseworker not only planned a person's rehab or return to the community, they provided drug cards, bus tickets, referrals to other agencies, as well as packing up the lockers of people who had not returned. They kept track of possessions so that the clients could return and retrieve their possessions within a certain time, and did all the documentation involved for the shelter and the city. This usually took two caseworkers and a housekeeper to maintain that kind of workload. Now it all fell to one caseworker, Virginia. This was the city's master plan so that eventually, the clients could live totally in independent living.

Trina from the Redemption Center facility was one of the people who were recruited for this new program. She was offered significantly more money but she would not work exclusively out of the Redemption Center. She would work out of a city office with the clients she had worked with and new clients, visiting them at whatever shelter they were staying in. She would try to divert them out of the shelter system and into housing administrated by the city.

During this time, the city felt that they had the right also to step in and check staff's credentials; even those who had been hired ten or fifteen years ago could be scrutinized. They could also dictate what qualifications they should have and if they were or were not fit to work in the new system that had been created. Trina was happy to leave the Redemption Center at that time, as most staff were. Would the city be better, however, or would they use her for a time and discard her? There was not a single staff that Mitch had met, however, including his former union partner who had not stated elation and a huge reduction in stress level at finally being freed from the Redemption Center. Trina was no different. The political game that you had to play in the city was a little different, though. You had to pretend to agree with their policies and not speak about the actual reality of what it was like to work with the clients. You had to be stifled, politically correct, and feign enthusiasm, which was not easy for a seasoned worker and Trina was outspoken at best.

Well, as the system continued to change, Mitch knew that his friend Nick D from the Jesus Saves Kitchen would be one of the casualties. As earlier mentioned, he got into a dispute with the twenty-one-year-old female worker fresh out of college about how to address and deal with abusive clients. Because Nick was not exactly the most politically correct person, the administration made mostly of women, sided with the female worker, citing that Nick was too rough with the clients.

It eventually led to his dismissal. Although Mitch urged him to get a lawyer and fight the policies with which he was dismissed, he refused to do it. This made Mitch sad at the whole state of the social work and nonprofit structure. Here was a man who had rehabbed and climbed up through the ranks for almost fifteen years and he was thrown on the scrap heap without even an explanation and was terminated with cause without severance or pay in lieu of notice. The fact was that he didn't fit in with the new concept of what social work/nonprofit was. The administration would claim that he was a casualty of the new accountability. But in reality, it had nothing to do with accountability whatsoever. He didn't fit in with the new concept because he was a dinosaur to all the new workers and as far as the all-female administration was concerned and that was the reality of the matter.

The clients loved it: Party time. The administration's ideas on the matter were a fallacy, hypocrisy, and the cruelest act perpetrated by a supposed empathetic social work system that Mitch had ever seen. Structure, including discipline, had to go hand in hand with empathy, and respect had to be earned if the client was to learn anything. The new order was to give it away for free as long as the beds stay full and the clients don't actually kill each other or staff.

Chapter Two

There was a lot of bad talk about unions around that time, mostly from administrators, CEOs, managers, or directors of companies or agencies. If there was anything that showed Mitch that unions were necessary for the common man, it was the sad saga of Nick. And Mitch had seen it so many times. Rather than fight, the employee would walk away with nothing because the employee was afraid to fight and knew they didn't have the money or the power to deal with a company that had a lawyer or several lawyers. The fact was that it was the fear factor. It's what companies used to chase people away and they knew that 99 percent of the time, an employee wouldn't challenge them because they didn't have the money or the wherewithal to stick with it until the end. The fact was, though, that you could challenge companies and in particular you could challenge charity organizations, especially those organizations that were not playing on the up and up themselves. If there's one thing that Mitch learned about these organizations, it was that they didn't want to be in the news any more than you did. This would shine the light on all the malfeasance, mistakes, and misappropriation that they had created. There were skeletons in everybody's closet including theirs.

The simple workingman was much better off with the union than without one. This was not what the administrators told you. It was not socialism or an excuse to overthrow the authority factor. It was a chance for employees and simple people to protect themselves. If you checked the history of unions, you would find that before unions were a reality, factory workers, women laborers, miners, and the people who built the railroads were worked to death and paid very little in compensation and if they should get hurt or sick or killed, there was no restitution for them or their families.

Now, of course, unions became a two-edged sword because along with the people who worked hard and just wanted protection and security, there were also those who took advantage of the union with absenteeism, sick time, refusal to do the amount of work required, and a general rebelliousness against the companies that employed them. But anything that is created for a good purpose is usually perverted and misappropriated. This is the reality of the world we live in.

In Mitch's experience, though, it was still better for the workingman to have a union than to not have one. The companies despised unions and had no respect for the worker. The worker was a drone and although they may be a paid slave, unlike times of old, they were still slaves and they could be replaced or they could be bumped or they could be unjustly disciplined without a union and that was the fact of the matter as far as Mitch had seen. He was very hurt and disillusioned by Nick's expulsion and that Nick was so intimidated by the status quo that he refused to fight. Mitch had his union battles both in the factory and in the social work world and he knew how to fight. As soon as you quoted laws, regulations, or employment standards, or labor laws to those in authority, they began to pay attention. There was a certain time back in Mitch's days at the New Apostles Center that he had barred a particularly dangerous client who had threatened him and thrown a tray of food at him. This was brought up at a general meeting with the administration and they agreed that this person should be barred. The next night, however, one of the monks (of the order) had let this person into the facility. Since this had happened many times before, Mitch refused to work with this person in the house. When Mitch refused to work, the executive director, Monk Jeff Davis, was brought in to confront Mitch. His comment was, "You will accept this decision and go to work now or you will be fired." Mitch's reaction was, "I have title and verse of the employment standards act here in my pocket, which states that I don't have to work with unsafe clients and that if you have been negligent in the administration of this situation, you are liable. You agreed to keep this client out and I will not work until he is. If you want me to go home, I will, but I will dispute this with the Labor Board and Human Rights Commission.

Monk Davis backed down and the monk responsible for letting this person in the house was reprimanded. By this time, Mitch knew a lot about unions and companies and the fear factor. Companies and agencies would try to scare you by threatening you with your livelihood but if you were in the right and had justice on your side, they usually backed down. They could not expose themselves to the same kind of scrutiny that they were exposing you to. The bright light of justice shines equally on the employer and the employee and in order to cast judgment, the employer must be as without blame as the employee. It was the employer's duty to make sure that the employee was safe. If there's one thing that Mitch learned during his Bible studies and Christian education, it was that fear is the opposite of faith. In fact, fear is faith corrupted. Fear was mostly a smoke show used by the administration to scare employees but if you were in the right and had the willingness to fight, you could let them know that we still lived in a civilized society and people still had rights.

With the Beasley Downtown Shelter (and drop-in center) closing down their overnight program and so many more clients in the building, several loose ends and weak spots within the system and within the staff began to become apparent. There were several incidents involving harassment by clients. The person who had been harassing Rita was back in the house. Ritchie was making a total pest of himself, fighting with other clients and showing up a late and drunk and flirting with Rita and other females on the desk, bordering on verbal abuse and assault and again, the agency did nothing about these issues. One night when Ritchie was in the house, a young man about the age of 22 entered the dorm Ritchie was staying in. Ritchie was drunk and lying down on his bed and had pretty well given it up for the night and was ready to go to sleep. This young man that we will call Tad walked into the dorm with his personal player and headphones playing a little too loud. When he lay down on his bed, those in the bunks surrounding him, including Ritchie, could hear every bit of his music coming from his headphones. Ritchie got up and approached Tad's bunk and without asking him to turn his personal player down, he simply smacked him as he was lying there.

Ritchie got a big surprise because Tad was a street-smart kid who knew how to fight. He got up from his bed and began punching and kicking Ritchie. In the first place, Ritchie was too old to deal with this young man who was in very good shape. Second, he was too drunk to deal with this young man. Tad beat him something brutal. He broke Ritchie's nose, a tooth and cut him up badly. Ritchie did not dare complain, being the tough guy that he was supposed to be. Rita was on duty and had to go up to the dorm and break up the fight. She did not bar the young man. In the first place, she hadn't seen the incident herself and secondly, she secretly thought it was about time that Ritchie got his due. Ritchie went to the hospital that night and was barred for drinking. Tad was allowed to remain.

Rita was having her adventures on shift lately, like the incident with Max Cassar. Here was a black fellow from Nigeria who liked white women a lot. He had some mental health issues that were quite serious. When a female worker was on the desk, he would just stand and stare at her. His attitude toward them was completely disrespectful, demeaning, and sexist. He had been warned many times but he was particularly fond of Debbie and Rita and he would flirt or just stare at them making obscene comments during snack time. Comments like, "I would like to see some of that whipped cream all over your face" were not uncommon. One Sunday, right during chapel service at noontime, Max was drunk and stoned when he returned to the center. Rita did not allow him in but he wanted his belongings, instantly. It was time for lunch and Rita could not leave the desk immediately. When Rita refused, he pulled his pants down, exposing his private parts. People coming in and out of chapel were insulted and indignant and asking what Rita was going to do about this problem. Again the misapprehension that the desk person was also a security guard and a bouncer existed, even if she was a female like Rita was. The employee who was Rita's partner that day was a new employee called Priscilla, better known as Mary Poppins, and she asked Max to leave the facility and return when he was sober and to pull his pants up.

At that Max took all his clothes off and began to parade around the lobby right during lunch food line and the comings and goings of the noontime chapel, absolutely naked. Because he was well endowed, he had a propensity to do this and this was not the first time he had done this kind of thing, although he had never done it in the shelter. Both Rita and Priscilla were flabbergasted and called police. When Max understood that they had called police, he left the facility and paraded out front naked. It was not long before he attracted quite the crowd. Just like people seeing someone on a ledge will say jump, some of the more radical members of society out front were clapping and egging Max on, asking him to dance, which he did. By the time police arrived, Max was putting on quite a show. It was sad, actually: another person with a mental-health issue without help or understanding. He was arrested and Rita and Priscilla had to make a report but as usual, the administration allowed him in again the next day.

This was one of the most frustrating things about being a frontline worker in nonprofit or social work. It didn't make it any easier that Priscilla, nicknamed Mary Poppins, had new worker syndrome times ten. With Debbie taking so much time off lately, it was Priscilla who filled in for her and as if things weren't complicated enough, her empathy and continual catering to the clients made life hell.

One of the things that Mitch had noticed about female caseworkers was that they were very competitive and very territorial. Each one wanted to be the most popular with the clients. Each one wanted to prove that their method of case management was the best, which was not always true. With longtime employee Annette out of the picture now, off sick most of the time and rarely able to work a full week, Rita had more or less taken over the desk, at least on day shift and weekends when Mitch was not around. Mitch's regular shift was still 4:00 to 11:00 weekday afternoons, the busiest shift. Because of Priscilla's innocence and tolerance toward the guys and her inability to see what they were really up to or set down boundaries for them, she made it difficult for other workers like Mitch to try and get any discipline imposed on the clients or any uniform structure. Book ins, the food line, snack time, and bed assignments were all total chaos. Every time Mitch went for break, you could be sure that Priscilla would sign in somebody that she shouldn't have, either someone that was barred, someone that was drunk, or someone that was totally unruly.

Mitch still got the odd call from Julie who was now a police officer. She had been through her training and successfully completed it. She soon wanted to come to Test City. That always had been her dream, to work with clients in the atmosphere that she had been trained for. She was sorry to hear the state that the Redemption Center had come to. She was also sorry for Mitch but there was little she could do. Mitch's wife, the godmother, began to really worry about Mitch. Mitch was now carrying these issues and these problems from the Redemption Center home with him. Not only did he have the clients to deal with and the administration, but also staff complaining to him constantly about union issues. Employees are sometimes very deluded when it comes to union issues. The general rule was that unless there was something in the collective agreement to deal with a union issue, there was no union issue.

Employees would call Mitch about personal battles between staff, about unfair practices when it came to work assignments, about what to do when administration would not cooperate on client issues. But in the end, unless it was an issue of ill treatment or dangerous working conditions, there was very little that Mitch could do except listen and it was draining him, little by little.

The godmother's advice was that union members and staff should not phone during Mitch's time off. If they needed questions answered, then phone him during work hours or arrange a time to talk during work hours because when it was time for him to be off, that was the time for him to recharge his batteries. Constant battering from above (the administration), from below from the clients, and from the side from the other staff was burning him out quickly.

Mitch still heard from Lou quite often also. She was little more than a paid lackey working for the New Apostles Center. As previously mentioned, she was everything from scrubwoman to a personal support worker, which should have never been her role. Her union was pretty ineffective when it came to dealing with these issues and she always found herself on the wrong side of the management when she questioned some of the duties that she was asked to do. Mitch had worked for the New Apostles Center in the past also and knew what they were capable of. They would put you in all kinds of precarious situations with clients yet when things went wrong, the employee always got the blame, and management always ran for cover. Lou Ann was unraveling quickly and Mitch helped her as much as he could with advice and ways to beat the administration through the union and the employment standards act while still maintaining her job and her dignity. He felt as bad for her as he had for his friend Nick and as Julie did for Mitch. Again, there was little anyone could do. And an incident had to happen or someone had to be hurt before the administration would act on these kinds of issues.

In the meantime, the administration, including Mr. Watson, had begun to really take a disliking to Debbie, mostly based on Stacey's opinion. Stacey's opinion was that Debbie didn't want to work. She was mostly not up in the case manager's office and was usually down on the desk helping Mitch with book-ins or the food line and generally not doing case management with clients. This wasn't totally accurate but it was their opinion. Rick had become firmly ensconced with Mr. Watson and Mr. Bain for that matter, even though he was still union rep and they were management. They saw in Rick that he was a man of his word and that he mostly didn't agree with a lot of the staff and the antics that went on. Mitch began to become quite concerned on a personal level that Rick was becoming a company man and he was very surprised at his development, considering that Rick been a union guy almost his whole life. In his factory days, he stood up for the issues that he believed in. Mitch probably stuck up a little too much for Debbie because of all this. a Debbie, however, tried to make the best of a situation that was impossible. To try and break things up for the guys a little bit, she did run events like card games, Halloween parties, pizza nights, and movie nights and it was a good thing, but the administration was not behind it at all—not financially and not morally.

This upset Debbie something awful and made her much more rebellious. Mitch, who was a staunch Christian, had a talk with Debbie one night, and just more or less said, "Debbie, you must protect yourself. You have to keep a low profile. Don't tell everyone what you think. Try keeping some things to yourself. Do what you need to do but don't inform them of everything that you do and don't argue with them. Let them think they're having their way."

The guys were all very impressed at the things that Debbie tried to do for them. She had an artistic flair, which made people think there was something special about her and in a way there was. Mitch had his own artistic gifts of music and writing but Mitch had also learned years ago, talent does not go hand in hand with character. Many people were blown away by someone's talent and the things that they could do to inspire others, but were they, themselves, in a position to inspire others?

The whole Hollywood experience displays what Mitch believed. Having the talent or ability to do something wonderful and to make a difference didn't mean that a person's character was ready for that. How many great stars, politicians, or other public figures had bit the dust through addictions, bad behavior, pride, or taking advantage of their position? Mitch's theory was that the only time that talent or ability to inspire others with a gift reached its apex was when the character of a person was equal to their talent. In other words, when the person was mature enough to take that talent and inspire others with it and be a good example themselves of what their talent displayed, mainly inspiration, integrity, and accountability. These things only came with full age, maturity, and knowledge. For these reasons, all the scriptural heroes were of full age before they were allowed to use their ministry or God-given gift. Moses was an old man in his seventies before his real ministry began. Abraham was in his eighties before he received his promise from the Lord to create a great nation through his son. Sampson, Solomon, and David were all fallible and fell short of the mark and made some grievous mistakes including adultery and murder. They were all redeemed in the end but it was a lesson that the gift to affect other people and inspire comes with full age.

Some of our modern examples made some grievous mistakes when they were put on the world stage before their character was of full maturity to be able to handle their gift.

Debbie had a wonderful gift for artistry and she could create fantastic display boards, displaying events, and decorations including cake decorating and room decorating, but she was very immature as far as her relations with people and the way she dealt with people and situations. Mitch had great hope for her, though. During one of their spiritual conversations, Debbie gave Mitch a rock that she had found when she traveled to Israel. It was from the Sea of Galilee and Jesus might have just walked on that rock. It became one of Mitch's most valued possessions and if he would remember Debbie for nothing else, he would remember her for that. His gift back to her was that he asked for a second rock and Mitch's wife, Jeanne, brought it to a jeweler, who drilled a hole through it and put it on a gold chain, which Mitch then presented to her for her birthday. Mitch prayed for her and had great hope for her, though he saw her seldom in the next little while. As previously mentioned, his new partner was Priscilla (Mary Poppins) who almost took Mitch to the end of his rope in those days and in the times that were to follow. Things were changing fast and Mitch was not part of the new order, nor did he want to be.

Chapter Three

Meanwhile, the word was that Stacey and Blain's relationship had reached epic proportions. This was becoming very sticky for Stacey because she was already being scrutinized for the way she dressed and some of the behavior she displayed with clients and staff. She was also very vindictive when it came to those who did not subscribe to her particular brand of social work. As previously mentioned, Blain spent long hours up in Stacey's office and other people besides Debbie and Mitch were starting to notice. Stacey was, in fact, becoming very friendly with all male staff. One day at the front desk area, she became very friendly with Rick and Mitch putting her arms around them and hugging them. That was also about the first time that Stacey had called Mitch into the med's room to talk. The med's room was like a small phone booth and there was not much room to maneuver.

Stacey with her low-cut tops, short dresses, and extremely touchy feely conversations made Mitch very nervous. It was a well-known fact that Mr. Bain would not even go into a closed office with a woman but especially with Stacey. He had an experience with a female staff saying things that were not true in the past.

It was a fact at one time a very good administrator called Mr. Brewster had run into the same Ms. Katie Farrell who had caused so much trouble at the Jesus Saves Kitchen. She was originally a manager at the Redemption Center but got fired for misappropriation of funds. She once accused Mr. Brewster of sexual harassment because he had said to her that she dressed somewhat inappropriately. Mr. Brewster was given no chance for defense but was simply transferred to another Redemption Center address. Eventually (after being the program director for a while) Ms. Farrell, who was fired from The Redemption Center, wound up at the Jesus Saves Kitchen where she eventually was fired for the same thing (after being program director there for a while). The point was that Mr. Brewster never stood a chance.

Mitch thought that these were some of the reasons that Mr. Bain and Mr. Watson gave Stacey so much latitude. They really did not want to confront Stacey or have to deal with the messy business of her then trying to level allegations against the Redemption Center. They had been through all that before. Since no one was paying attention or questioning Stacey on these issues, including her falling asleep at meetings or being caught incoherent or unresponsive during a working day, she became more brazen. She was addicted to antidepressants, and her familiarity with clients and staff and the alleged romance with Blain became more careless and Stacey took more chances. She and her friends Eva and Katie T had now made a weekly habit of going out to bars, leaving their cars in the parking lot and picking them up later. They supposedly met with several clients and went out dining and drinking with these people. Blain became much more brazen, also figuring he could break the rules as far as curfews, coming home under the influence, and bragging to his other client friends that if you got in good with the administrator, you could do whatever you wanted in the shelter. It certainly seemed that way because anytime that there was an issue with Blain or his behavior, Stacey simply ignored it and he was allowed to continue what he was doing.

The rumors about Blain and Stacey had become so widespread that the federal parole officers from the third floor had mentioned it to Mitch and the union and even to Mr. Bain and Mr. Watson, the administrators. The administration again had totally ignored the situation and continued to ignore it. When Mitch and the union people, with a petition signed by all the staff, approached Mr. Bain and Mr. Watson on these issues again, the proof was not conclusive as far as they were concerned. It seemed that half the city and all the workers were privy to the situation and the only people that weren't paying attention were the administration and it became very frustrating. Further, the fact that Mitch and the union had started a petition to inform the administration of what Stacey was up to still bore no fruit.

Staff officers and clients from federal parole continued coming to Mitch and stating their concerns about this situation because Stacey was also meeting with probationary clients and it was becoming a real concern for the security and respectability among probationary clients and the shelter administration. The parole employees, including detectives and probationary officers, became more vocal and even went to Mr. Bain and Mr. Watson and still the situation was ignored.

When these issues occur, it enables and empowers the clients to be braver. Now clients thought they could hit on any staff and that the only thing that would occur was that they might be questioned by the administration who they realized were blind to the actual frontline experience. Several of these issues were coming to a head at the same time, it seemed: the probationary employees from the third floor complaining about Stacey's relationships, Debbie who was officially the caseworker claiming to Mr. Bain and Mr. Watson that Stacey's personal relationship with Blain was inappropriate, and the new person who entered the scene, who was a Canadian graphic artist of some reputation whose name was John Cameron. John had met Stacey at some bar and had asked her out. Stacey had been dating John on and off even though she had a continuing relationship with Blain. The reckoning finally came when John asked Stacey to marry him. They were only three months into the relationship. Stacey had already been through a messy divorce before she came to the Redemption Center, partially for the lifestyle that she displayed while working there. She liked to go out to bars, to party, to sing karaoke, and was very promiscuous especially when drinking, but John Cameron fell head over heels for her.

While Stacey would like nothing more than to be married to someone, especially someone of prominence, this created a problem because Blain was head over heels for Stacey and wouldn't let go. Now Stacey had the problem of trying to release herself from Blain without devastating him and without his angry response, which might be to tell all he knew about her.

Katie T and Eva were quite aware of all these circumstances but with all the special privileges they received for being Stacey's friend, which included leaving work early, going for lunches and drinks during working hours, having parties together, and going out with clients, they were not about to ruin their situation. In other words, the usual rules the caseworkers had to follow did not apply to them. There came a certain night when in the ninth degree of brazenness, Stacey, Katie, and Eva proved themselves to be in total disregard of rules. Clients and staff knew it but still not the administration.

On a certain Saturday night, there was a part-time employee on the desk whose name was Rusty. Rusty was a young black fellow, approximately twenty-five years old. He was a martial arts expert and going through school to study law or to try to become a police officer. He was usually very stern with clients and other staff. He would put up with no slight from anyone, yet for some reason, he was intimidated by Stacey, either because of her position or because he had a soft spot for her—it was hard to say.

On this particular night, Katie T and Eva entered the Redemption Center front desk area. It was obvious that they'd been drinking and drinking quite a bit. They were slurring their words and staggering. They began flirting with Rusty and he was enamored of it all. They were there for a particular purpose, however, and their purpose was to see if Blain was in his room. They wanted to go up and knock on his door and retrieve him. To request this was beyond belief but incredibly, Rusty allowed them into the facility after hours and under the influence and allowed them to knock on Blain's door to see if he was available. Eva could be very persuasive. "Please, Rusty, we don't want to hurt him or bug him. We just want to ask him some questions. Is that okay? We won't cause any trouble or wake anybody up, we promise." Katie T chimed in, "We are just helping him. He's supposed to go into one of these new apartments provided by the city and we want to work out some details with him, if that's okay?"

So against all policy, Rusty allowed Eva and Katie T into the facility. They should have known that this was all being viewed on surveillance camera, but they were too drunk to care. Unlike what they told Rusty, they did make an inordinate amount of noise knocking on the door to wake Blain up. Blain had already gone to bed because he had to be up at 6:00 a.m. for work at 8:00.

When they could not arouse him, they began talking louder and calling his name. They woke half of the permanent residents in the rooms so that they were peeking out their doors to see what was going on. Finally, Blain came to the door half asleep. Blain had received a job recently with the help of Debbie and he was really trying to stay clean, at least as far as the crack was concerned, and limiting his drinking to when he was off on weekends. Katie T and Eva convinced him that they needed to talk to him outside. They all walked from the building and headed out the back parking lot and down the alley to Ward Street. There was a long-distance surveillance camera that reaches the street. There, waiting for them on the street in her car, was Stacey. When they reached the car, Eva and Katie T got into the back seat and Blain got in the front seat with Stacey. They kissed immediately. Apparently after that, they went out for a wild night on the town, hitting several bars, going to some places where Stacey could sing karaoke, and there was even a rumor that after Stacey dropped Katie and Eva off that Stacey and Blain went to a motel for the night. Even though it was the weekend, Blain still had to work. He arrived home at five o'clock in the morning and had to be at work at eight.

Rather than acting sheepishly, he walked in quite cocky and confident and Rita, who was on the desk at that time, did notice that he was completely drunk and stoned and reported it in the log and made an incident report, although she allowed him into his room. He grabbed his gear for work and went to work. How he managed, it was hard to fathom, but he did. That night, he did not return from work. Word was that he met with Stacey again and spent the Sunday the same way he'd spent the Saturday night in a motel room, drinking, using drugs, and having sex with Stacey.

On the Monday morning that followed, Rusty and Rita felt a responsibility to report what they had seen to Mr. Bain and Mr. Watson. Katie T and Eva were called in to the office. Stacey was mysteriously absent on that Monday. The meeting with Katie T, Eva, and Mr. Watson was a fact-finding mission and therefore union representation was not necessary, though they could have asked. When Mitch came to work for his afternoon shift on Monday, he received a strange call at about 7:00 p.m. It was a call from Eva who began to tell Mitch all the things that had been going on. Eva and Mitch had no rapport and Mitch knew that this call was simply because Eva, Katie T, and perhaps Stacey were in a lot of trouble and she wanted to talk to someone and she knew that eventually she would need union representation.

"Mitch," she said. "There are things that have been going on that I should tell you about. Stacey has been drinking with the clients and going out with them. She and Blain have been having an affair; she's even been having sex with him up in her office. Katie and I just went out with them. We didn't have anything to do with drinking or sleeping with clients. The agency knows that we came here on the weekend looking for Blain and they want answers. I'm asking if you would come in with us and talk for us if there is discipline."

Mitch's answer was, "This is all new material to me. I have no idea of what's going on. Since you work with Rick more than you work with me, perhaps it's better if you used him as your union steward."

Eva's reply was, "You're a rep for the union and we would rather use you. I feel helpless in this situation, I know that we have not had a great relationship in the past but this is serious and I could lose my job. I want to come clean about Stacey and what she's been doing."

Mitch's reply was, "No matter what our relationship was, I will do my job as the union rep to advocate for you and protect you as far as the collective agreement, union rules, and policy and procedure are concerned."

Mitch had no illusions about what Eva had said. He was sure that she and Katie T were involved as much as Stacey. They got Blain out of the building that night when Rusty was on duty to bring him to Stacey so that Stacey and he could go off together and although Katie T usually did not fraternize with clients,

Mitch was pretty sure that Eva had. Mitch had thought that it was all to placate Blain by having a last fling with him so that when Stacey broke up with him, he would not be too devastated.

The next day, Tuesday, Stacey finally showed up to work. Mr. Bain and Mr. Watson called her into the office and questioned her on the fact that Eva and Katie T had been called in and spoken to and had admitted that Blain was retrieved from the building by them for Stacey and that Blain was seen getting into her car by the surveillance camera. She denied culpability. She denied that they were drinking or that they stayed in a motel room, and claimed that all the things that Eva and Katie T were saying were to protect themselves. The rats were jumping ship and it was obvious that in the end, the person who would be holding the bag would be Stacey. Debbie was furious that all the work she had done with Blain seemed to be for naught and that Stacey could get away with such antics and the administration still stonewalled and pretended that it wasn't happening or couldn't believe that it could happen.

"How does this fucking bitch get away with this shit?" was Debbie's statement. Her frustration had reached epic proportions.

Julie, who still called Mitch when she could (now being a police officer and very busy), could not believe the things that were going on at the Redemption Center. "I miss you, Mitch, but I don't miss that place. It's a zoo. I hope you get out of there soon, for your sake."

Mitch's wife, Jeannie, the godmother's comments were more caustic and to the point. "I've never seen a place that is more thoughtless of employees and the clients and less proactive when it comes to dealing with situations. What a Mickey Mouse organization"—which was absolutely true. Meanwhile, as earlier mentioned, many employees had left or were on sick leave. Annette, the old desk person who had originally been the rep of the union and the one who trained most people on the desk, was now too sick to come in more than a day or two a week. She would eventually go off altogether. Her husband, the maintenance man at the Redemption Center for twenty years, was retiring, also. He could have stayed but decided to leave considering the changes that were now happening and Annette now permanently off sick. Eva and Katie were also on their way out the door. That was as sure as Julie and Debbie and Lou Ann who had left. Mitch's old-time union partner, Cindy, and Trina M had left.

Mitch was starting to feel like the only person left on a sinking ship. It was obvious, also, that the administration did not want Mitch there. In fact, it was obvious that the administration did not want a union at all. When Mitch had first taken his position as union rep, he was voted in by 98 percent, displacing a person called Mary who was apparently a company person and did not advocate for the staff. She would not help or put in grievances, however legitimate, for union people in trouble. She was supposedly in the company's pocket. Word was that the administration was leaning toward her to replace Mitch. Mitch wanted things like security for the Redemption Center, security guards as protection for staff, more stringent penalties for clients, and a more open atmosphere with counseling and debriefing for clients and staff.

The administration, spurred on by the city, wanted one thing and one thing only—housing of clients—and it didn't matter what offense they had committed. Keep the shelter full and no service restriction of clients unless approved by the administration and then the offense must be serious enough to merit a service restriction of more than 24 hours.

There was another issue happening at this point. Mitch was beginning to have some physical problems. These problems were partially based on the stress level he was having through the work situation. Mitch was 56 years old and not a kid anymore. While most people lasted five years in frontline social work, Mitch had lasted 18 years and as well as being the rep of the union, he had been a manager, supervisor, off-site supervisor, coordinator, as well as an addictions counselor and a caseworker.

With all the changes to the system lately, his tolerance was running thin. He found himself less able to deal with the clients on an increasing basis. He was unable, anymore, to be tolerant of their stories and their antics. He took the advice of his good friend, Nick. "You can't help all the clients or change the system. Pick yourself one or two who have potential and try to help them." Mitch had always tried to do that, but he tried to do that more now, focusing on that and his Christian beliefs to get him through the experiences he was going through with the crumbling system. It was becoming hard to keep perspective. He was now having some heart palpitations and he felt the stress was elevating his blood pressure and causing some stomach issues. Many days, he would be full of anxiety hours before he had to actually go to work. He was not sleeping well or eating well, either. The good relationship that he had had with Mr. Watson and Mr. Bain had become completely frayed.

Now that Julie was gone, Rick was becoming more and more a company man, also, and with Debbie there only part of the time, Mitch had to work with Priscilla (Mary Poppins) many a night, which caused him a world of grief. He wound up many times in a house full of drunken, stoned, and disorderly clients and a worker who catered to their every need or want, preparing fancy platters for snack, full of delicacies that she could find around the center, many times using food that they would have used for meals the next day, giving clients extra dinners, extra desserts, extra privileges, late passes, and pretty well anything they asked for. It was beyond belief and it empowered the clients to the point where they thought they were running the center and not the staff.

The administration seemed to have totally lost track of what was going on. After Stacey's little talking to on the Tuesday of that week, she had taken a four-day hiatus, claiming sick. What happened next finally dissolved the glue that held the frontline and the administration in some kind of cohesive order. It was mayhem and it was the end of a certain era and the beginning of another, where people like Mitch simply would not belong anymore.

Chapter Four

The date was finally set for John and Stacey's wedding. There was no one on the planet who Stacey had not told. It was touted to be a gala affair. It seemed during that period that Blain was going to visit Stacey in her office much more often. His need for counseling had escalated by 98 percent. Around this time, Blain began drinking and using crack much more frequently. Stacey had the problem of keeping Blain placated while she was trying to get her wedding plans under way. Her fiancé, John, was having a showing of his work at the Redemption Center chapel. Quite a few people (staff, clients, and outsiders) showed up to see it. Fortunately, Blain was absent that night. John, the fiancé, had no idea about Blain or the relationship that had developed between him and Stacey. Stacey was only a year out of another divorce and had to vacate her house in order that it could be sold. The proceeds were split between her and her former husband. She and her teenage son moved in with John. Otherwise Stacey would have been homeless at that point. Still, Blain pursued her. She had been foolish enough to originally give him her home number, cell phone number, and her address. Mitch, on duty one afternoon shift, got another strange call from Eva.

"I feel guilt. I have been a part of this whole thing between Stacey and Blain. I don't know what to do at this point. I have some stress issues and I'm having a nervous breakdown and I can't keep things a secret anymore. I don't want to go to the administration. Stacey's still a friend of mine but I can't stand by and watch what she's doing any more."

Mitch knew it was all lies from one end to the other. She had already been to the administration and she was just now trying to cover her butt, seem repentant, and get Mitch on her side.

Mitch's reply was, "The administration will not listen to complaints of these types unless they see it with their own eyes. My advice is to protect yourself at this point and get your story straight for when they call you in."

As previously mentioned, Mr. Watson had become increasingly hard on the employees. The new city mandate allowed clients in at whatever cost and turned a blind eye to the behavior going on in the shelter. Mitch was under fire and so was the union. Mr. Watson and Mr. Bain had stopped communicating with Mitch on the issues happening at the center, whether it was staff or clients.

Rick had become his go-to guy now and Mitch was convinced that breaking the union was Mr. Watson's focus. Mitch also had to take more time off because of health issues. Mitch now had chronic hypertension, a stress disorder, and some angina. He was ordered by his doctor to reduce his hours to three days a week. This did not please Mr. Watson at all. When Mitch turned in his doctor's note, Mr. Watson's reply was, "This is going to make life very difficult for us. We now have to fill your shift and having Fridays off as one of your days is not an option. We've tried to do a lot for you in the past but it doesn't seem as though one hand is washing the other here."

Mitch's reply was, "Whatever you did for me in the past has nothing to do with this conversation and should not be brought up as if there was something I could do about my medical situation. Your attitude seems to protect Redemption Center and the continuing operation of it without any regard for the employee."

Mr. Watson said, "You're the one that has muddied the waters." Mitch's reply was, "We better not discuss this anymore."

Rick was in the office, also, during this conversation and did not offer any input to the right or left but kept silent. Mitch was becoming increasingly disappointed with Rick and his company attitude. He was always making these broad statements that he was in no one's pocket and that he was a union man at heart, but it seemed at this point he was just taking care of the bottom line, not that he made a lot of money, but Mitch was sure that it helped supplement his pension from the factory that he had worked for.

Rick and Mitch had been so tight at one time. Now, it would seem as though Rick had made an abrupt change. As there was no basis for conversation anymore and it seemed as though Rick always kept silent or took the company's side, Mitch realized that because of his illness he was a liability. Mitch missed that friendship. It came to the same conclusion that most—except the very few—had come to. Rick was just like every other close friend or mentor he had ever known. When it came to dollars and cents, dollars and cents won every time.

Annette was off sick and she phoned Mitch one shift for an update. Mitch knew that with Annette's physical problems, she was not likely to return, especially in light of the new situation that was happening at the Redemption Center. About that time, there was a union-management meeting in which some of the city mandates and the new rules and regulations regarding this were discussed with the union. Mr. Watson had proclaimed that Mr. Bain and he and the administration had magnanimously decided to hire an extra staff person at the front desk since the hospital release program was closing and Rick could no longer be part of that operation. Mr. Watson made it very clear that the extra person was not to be on the desk with desk staff or helping during dinners or with book ins. This second person was to monitor dorms and the TV room to make sure there was no trouble or mischief among the clients and to talk and connect with clients. His attitude was that of a little Napoleon and he said that there would be ramifications and discipline for employees who spent too much time talking at the front desk and did not comply with this new edict.

Mitch thought this was extreme and uncalled for and stated such. "We're not small children and do not have to be told what to do every minute. If help is needed on the desk, the extra person was always the person who chipped in to help. Now that there is no caseworker on shift, we would expect that this extra person would continue with this additional help when needed."

Mr. Watson's reply was, "I think you're being very childish; it has just been pointed out what our focus for this new position is."

Mitch's reply was, "There is a veiled threat that includes discipline, and this is not necessary for you to explain what the new job will be."

A little previous to this time, because of Mitch's health and his reduced hours, he knew he could not continue as full-time union rep. Because there was no one else who would offer to help (with the exit of both Cindy and Debbie), Mitch went to the former rep whom he had defeated in the last election, Mary. Mary was a crusty, small, not very attractive lady who had been ousted from her union position originally because it was perceived by the staff that she was in the company's pocket and would not advocate for members. Yet she had many times stirred the pot when Mitch had to tell certain clients that they did not have a legitimate case. Whenever a personal dispute between staff would happen (these were not union issues), Mary sent these people to Mitch just to make Mitch's life miserable. She had a married friend and co-worker named Shareen who was constantly giving her advice and stirring the pot. When Mitch's health was to the point that he knew that he could not handle the union thing anymore, he stepped out and left Mary in charge—at least she had done the job before. When the next election came, if the staff were not happy with her, they could replace her at that time.

Rick again stayed silent during this revelation and during most other interactions between the company and Mitch at this time. Meanwhile, during that time, staff was quitting, there were clients in crisis, and because of the city's change in the shelter system, it became increasingly difficult to go to work. You never knew if your replacement would show up and you didn't know what you would be dealing with from day to day: fights, addictions, ambulances, overdoses, and staff disputes. The absenteeism was the huge issue. If your relief didn't show for their shift, the administration expected you to work a double and further, if you didn't, they were upset with you. Mitch became increasingly despondent and stressed because of the circumstances at the center and received more calls from Rita, Annette, Eva, and

Katie T, all in crisis. Most of them had already taken significant time off looking for other jobs.

Rita was getting called into the office often for telling clients exactly what she thought, in other words, not taking abuse from clients, but rather responding. She was having arguments with the more lazy confrontational staff, also. She had a big fight on the desk with Eva one day. This argument was based on the fact that Eva thought that because she was a caseworker she didn't have to do any work. She thought her only job was to counsel clients and not even to keep notes on that. All her paperwork fell to whoever would be on the desk. But with Rita doing her own work and Eva's, it began to become a little much, especially since Eva would take hour and a half lunch break and Rita was left holding the bag. The time came when Rita let Eva have it in a showdown on the desk, calling her a slacker and a liar because she had maligned a former worker Tammy who had done a very good job. She said that the reason that she could not do a good job was because Tammy had not left her proper notes or had left the office in disarray. This was a complete fabrication because Tammy was very specific about her job and had integrity in it. It was an excuse because Eva simply could not do the job. She liked to spend hours with clients in a session that should've taken fifteen minutes and as a result, her other work was not done. At this point, when the company again sided with Eva, Rita found it a little too much to take and went off sick claiming a physical problem but actually the problem was stress. Like many other employees, she felt unable to speak her peace to the administration. The administration was famous for not getting involved in the day to day issues that happened at the shelter, not getting their hands dirty with the fights and hassles. In the meantime, invitations went out for the big stag and doe party for Stacey and John to take place at her new fiancés home in an affluent suburb of the city. From all reports, it was a drunken party with karaoke, a lot of gossiping, and it was quite the scandal when reported by staff the next day. Clients, of course, were not invited. It was the one smart thing Stacey did during that period.

Blain was now going to Debbie on a regular basis, when Debbie was working, to tell Debbie the whole story of him and Stacey and how Stacey had jilted him because she now had a prominent fiancé. It seemed to Blain that her affections were based on money not love. This put Debbie in a precarious position. She could not go to the administration and she could not demean or slander Stacey and have it come back to her. So she comforted Blain to the best of her ability but during a conversation with Mitch, she let him know exactly how she felt. "Why doesn't she just leave him alone? He's got problems of his own and the only reason she went after him was sex and now she is ruining him. He lost his job, he's back to the crack and the drinking, and he's a mess. He is emotionally broken and it's her fault. Isn't there anything we can do to set it right, Mitch?"

Mitch's reply was, "It won't do any good. Even a blind man could see what is going on but not this administration, even though it's reaching epic proportions. All we can do is wait, hold our breath, and get through this."

Mitch was plain about the fact that he didn't care for Blain. Blain had been cocky and arrogant about his position with Stacey and resented Mitch's disapproval of the situation and the questions Mitch asked when he came home late or under the influence or bragging about his relationship with Stacey. This did not interfere with Mitch's impartiality, however. And during a conversation with Blain, Mitch's input was, "You could be doing so much more. You have the potential to be whatever you want. You're smart and articulate and you have a conscience, unlike many others who come through here. I just don't want to see you go down in flames because of someone else." No names were mentioned but Blain knew exactly what was meant.

After the stag and doe, wedding plans became all consuming for Stacey. She had taken some holidays, and they had gone off to the Dominican Republic before the actual wedding. This news made Blain feel even more disenfranchised. During this time, Blain was finally approved for an apartment through the city placement program. As long as he continued to work and stay straight, Welfare would continue to subsidize his housing until he was on his feet. Blain kept after Stacey, however, with phone calls, visits, and going to Eva and Katie T to try and get access to Stacey. She was ignoring him until one night, Stacey felt she could no longer ignore the situation and had to resolve it once and for all. Claiming to John to be going out with Katie T and Eva, she planned to get Blain out of the building and talk to him. That was the night that it all hit the fan and there was no denying any more from the administration standpoint, union, staff, or clients. It was finally obvious. Blain came home drunk, bragging he'd spent the night with Stacey. Stacey was off for several weeks and no one knew her status. She apparently was being reviewed by the administration. On the day when they called her in for their fact finding meeting and to decide her status, they met in another building apart from the Redemption Center Shelter but still on the property. The minutes of the meeting were related by other sources and the buzz went through the center like a shockwave.

Chapter Five

The meeting consisted of Mr. Bain (HR), Mr. Watson (Exec. PD), Stacey (PD), and Sarah M. (administrative assistant and recording secretary.) Mr. Watson began, "Stacey, I simply can't ignore these rumors any longer. So the question is, have you been seeing the client Blain after hours and if so, was it strictly on a professional basis or is there something more that we should know about?" Stacey's response was, "I must admit that I have taken a personal interest in Blain and I will be honest; we have been out for dinner and even a few drinks on occasion."

Mr. Bain chimed in at that point, "Were Katie T or Eva or any other clients involved at these meetings?" Stacey's response was, "I cannot divulge this information. It would be up to you to question the others on these issues."

Mr. Bain responded again, "I'm afraid, Stacey, that this time you have gone farther than we can sanction. What did you would think would happen when you broke the rules of confidentiality and intimacy with a client?"

At that point, Mr. Bain asked for an adjournment while he spoke to Mr. Watson and Sarah in another room. Stacey was asked to wait. It was only fifteen minutes or so before all three returned with a verdict. Mr. Watson did the speaking, "I'm afraid, Stacey, we cannot allow you to continue here under the circumstances. We would caution you not to repeat this behavior in the future. We will, however, not withhold a generic but positive reference for you and you will also be paid severance and pay in lieu of notice and your separation papers will read that your position has been replaced because of restructure. We would hope there would be no animosity or hurt feelings. In many ways, you did a very good job. You crossed the line, however, with the client/worker relationship. We wish you good fortune in the future."

Stacey silently accepted the verdict and walked out. With an impending marriage and a reference, she was okay with it. She wanted out at that point, anyway. Her two friends had betrayed her and the place was going to hell in a hand basket anyway—time to move on.

The administration waited three weeks to inform the union and the staff that Stacey had been terminated and details were not revealed. It was simply stated that it was mutually agreed that it was time for Stacey to move on and that her job would be replaced and restructured. The administration would be going with a manager instead of a PD, a working manager, in other words. This seemed like very good news to the union and the staff. Katie T and Eva began taking even more time off than they had in the past and were now accountable for their workload. Mr. Watson started to take on more demands on the front desk, also, and the only caseworker left other than Virginia was Trina T who would soon be gone also—one caseworker for 120 clients and strictly on day shift. After the incident of Stacey's termination, apparently a big fight happened with her and fiancé, John. John had somehow found out why she was terminated and this was obviously not new information. This was part of the reason that her first marriage collapsed: her promiscuity and her inability to draw lines of structure in counseling and social work.

John, of course, made a huge issue out of it and called off the impending engagement. Stacey went into a frantic rage and destroyed John's house while he was at work, smashing the TV, stereo, lamps, his bar, and several other items. John called the police when he returned and had her removed from the premises because when he had returned home from work, she had attacked him also, giving him a black eye and a bloody nose. At that point, Stacey placed her son with relatives and moved into a motel room for the time being. None of this information was known by staff or clients, now that Stacey was no longer an employee of the Redemption Center.

Mitch took no pleasure in the downfall of others and he prayed for her. Her past had to be a consideration in all this. Apparently, Stacey had been very overweight at one time, had suffered a lot of ridicule, and had a self-esteem issue. She had worked hard to lose the weight and now appeared quite attractive. Instead of being happy and settled with the accomplishment, she wanted to prove that she was the sexiest woman in her fifties that anyone had ever seen, with the low-cut cleavage, short dresses, and too much eye makeup. This was all to prove that she had arrived and was a cry for attention. These are the wrong reasons to do these things and these cries for attention only proved a lack of self-esteem. Stacey was not doing well, drinking in a motel room, spinning out of control. She lost her fiancé and her job in one fell swoop. She had no thought of what she had done to Blain, however.

There was no one to go to. All her so-called friends like Eva and Katie T had all abandoned Stacey when she lost her job at the Redemption Center and she was very confused and without direction. The administration, of course, would not admit its own complicity in all this by ignoring it for so long. In fact, behind closed doors, they said that they would not discuss this with the union because the union would say "we told you so." The fact was, though, that Mitch and the union had told them so. Their official stance was that this was a management issue and therefore nothing to do with the union. The fact was that these kinds of incidents happened in every agency that Mitch had ever worked in. Crossing the line was quite common in the social work field. These kinds of statistics were not widely known, however. One thing about all of these agencies was that they did not want negative publicity about their agency, even if it didn't have anything to do with them personally because this would then shine the light on the organization itself and if any malfeasance was going on from an administration standpoint (and many times it was), they would be scrutinized also. When it came to life, they were fallible the same as clients and staff were. And the longer someone was a worker, the more chinks became apparent in their armor.

Mitch began getting more and more calls from Eva. She was now worried that she would be next to go. Eva and Katie T both got off the hook, however. They knew their days were numbered and as well as taking a lot of time off, they both began in earnest to look for other work. It came out later that Eva and Katie T were actually the ones who told the administration about Stacey and what she was doing with Blain when they were called in, several weeks back. Stacey's best friends had betrayed her, and as well as the situation with her job and her fiancé, it was a little too much to take. When all of her friends had abandoned her, she sat in her motel room drinking and taking downers. Eventually, there was no one else to turn to except for Blain and that's what she did one fateful night. So Stacey called Blain in tears, distraught, drunk, and stoned, and asked if she could come over to his new place. As previously mentioned, Blain was now in subsidized housing provided by the city. There were some strict rules of occupancy (one was no overnight guests) although they were rarely followed. Stacey snuck in that night and no one saw her. She brought plenty of supplies: downers, painkillers, and booze. Blain already had some crack and pot. Taking painkillers and downers like valium was also a common thing that Stacey and Blain did. They took some downers and started drinking.

"I love you, Stacey," was Blain's statement and Stacey said, "I don't know what I'm going to do with my life now." They made love on the little single bed Blain had in his apartment. It was a simple bachelor, all one room, bed at one end and the kitchen at the other. They didn't feel that they were stoned enough and at that point, they took some painkillers and crack as well.

After making love a couple of times, Blain was feeling nauseous and had bed spins. He got up to try to go to the bathroom to be sick but he never quite made it. Stacey had fallen asleep by this time. Blain vomited in the middle of the living room but continued on to the bathroom and was there for quite some time leaning over the toilet. On his way back from the bathroom, Blain slipped on the vomit that was in the middle of the living room. He fell and split his head open. He lay there for quite some time until Stacey had to go to the bathroom, approximately 4:00 a.m. When she found Blain in the middle of the floor, she tried to revive him without success. Blain was dead. Police were called and Stacey was brought in for questioning.

Because some of the workers in third floor parole were police, Mitch found out about this. Before that, however, Eva had phoned Mitch again on an afternoon shift and told him Blain was dead. All of this information had come from Stacey but no one knew what the real truth of the matter was. The fact was that only a week before in a violent rage, Stacey had pretty well demolished John's house. Stacey was apparently questioned for several days and although released, told not to leave town because there might be further questioning.

It was, of course, the talk of the center and of parole. Mitch was honest about his feelings about Blain. Mitch had never thought Blain was a client who would be successful reintegrating himself into society. In fact, the whole subsidized housing experiment was to try to get the statistics to make it look like off-site housing was a huge success, so that they could eventually shut the shelters down—exactly as they had done with mental health issues and the mental health act shutting down mental health facilities. Debbie went into a huge spin over the death of Blain, claiming that if she was still his worker and Stacey had never taken him on as a client, this would never have happened. She cried and carried on over Blain for several weeks. "Why didn't she just fucking leave him alone? She toyed with him and now he's dead and she's responsible."

The administration of the Redemption Center did not even acknowledge the death of Blain to the employees or the situation. As far as they were concerned, Stacey was no longer an employee of Redemption Center and as such there was no culpability on their part. Of course, people love a train wreck and the talk about Stacey continued for months and her reputation was infamous. Mitch postulated that if this was a male staff that had done this, he would be in jail no matter what the circumstances.

Eva again called Mitch one afternoon shift and asked if Stacey had come to speak to him about the situation that was going on. Mitch's response was, "Stacey doesn't work here anymore and as such, I've been informed by the administration that she is not allowed on the property and since she is not union but management, I don't know what I could possibly do for her." Eva went to Rick instead because at this point, he was still a union steward. She did not dare go to Debbie, even though she was also a union steward. There was no love lost between them. Rick gave her no satisfaction either. It seemed that now that Stacey was in trouble, all of a sudden Katie T and Eva had nothing to do with the incidences involving clients.

Many a staff came to Mitch during that period asking what was going on, including the parole employees and clients upstairs. Mitch only knew what he had heard and felt it inappropriate to relate gossip. Mitch had certainly been the subject of that kind of thing before when he himself crossed the line in the past and understood what it meant when people were gossiping about you and embellishing the facts. Sometimes you empathize or advocate for a client and can't help because the system doesn't work. It led to a tendency to bend and even break the rules and sometimes step over the line and get lost in whatever ensuing drama is taking place with the clients.

Meanwhile, the Redemption Center was again without a program director. The clients took this as an opportunity to take advantage of the situation with more addictions, drunkenness, and fighting. The administration was still trying to piece together what was left of the center and had no time for staff complaints on these issues. Mitch's comment at the union-management meeting was that eventually there would have to be armed security at the door to assure safety for the staff and clients. Again, this notion was fluffed off and not taken seriously. Mr. Watson and Mr. Bain took a more active role in the running of the center while they were looking for another PD. They brought in a former manager from another agency, part of the Redemption Center crew. This manager took responsibility for the kitchen and maintenance staff while Mr. Bain and Mr. Watson kept an eye on the front desk and the one remaining caseworker. Stacey was eventually not scrutinized by police anymore and Blain's death was ruled an accident. She found another job in addictions and was still part of social work in

Test City—She was also reconciled with her fiancé and eventually married, beyond belief.

Many more workers quit during that period and the reality was that the place scared most workers to death. The administration did not debrief the workers or clients. It was more typical administration stonewalling and arrogance. Debbie carried a torch for Blain for a long time. It was the third client she had worked with who had died and at least ten that she had known had gone back to the street. With the cuts and layoffs, through the union she had a right to apply for night shift on the desk. With her record of absenteeism, however, having small children and having to leave in the middle of shifts and during crisis situations, she was warned by the administration that she must attend work and stay for the whole shift unless it was a proven and documented emergency. At that, Debbie decided not to stay and took a layoff. Until Trina's date came to go to the city, she became Mitch's partner and although she had some experience and was supportive, there was no camaraderie, debriefing, or fun on their shift.

Chapter Six

So as if the situation was not bad enough, Mitch's afternoon shifts became very boring when there wasn't trouble and Trina was very little help as a partner, not from a working standpoint as much as from a relationship standpoint. Trina basically did her thing and Mitch did his. When she came down to relieve him for break, she was always rushing him along; she just wanted to get it over with. There was no banter or conversation between them. She would talk about her relationship with her boyfriend and her particular thoughts about the center but she was not interested in anyone else's life or perspective. About that time, many things began to happen in rapid succession. As previously mentioned, most of the programs were canceled, which meant the layoffs of nurses, the nurse practitioner, and all the case managers. Mitch's new partner in the union, Mary, was not much help either.

About that time, one of the clients from the off-site housing project began to come around the center to eat dinner and snack and try to access the programs. He usually came drunk and stoned out of his mind. One particular day, Mitch would not allow him entrance. After a heated argument in which he called Mitch every name in the book, spitting on Mitch as he spoke even through the slats of glass, he became angrier when Mitch would not allow him in for evening snack. In the first place, he was not a resident of the center and secondly he was too drunk to enter. He kept at Mitch until Mitch threatened to call the police. At this point, the man, Luis Escobar, punched the tempered glass of the front desk bubble. Although it was not bulletproof glass, it was tempered glass and it was meant to repel attacks and keep violent clients from getting at staff. Luis punched the glass and instead of breaking it, his fist smashed like a pancake getting blood all over himself, Mitch, and everything on the front desk area including the nightly reports.

Mitch felt it his responsibility to phone the off-site housing worker who was connected with the center as well as the police. Mitch thought that they should know that their client was going to be arrested and to discuss the matter of his continuing patronage at the center, even though he didn't live there anymore. The response was somewhat cold and the head of the department, Jessie Ann, made an appearance at the center even though Luis had already been arrested. Instead of taking him to jail, however, the police had taken him back to his apartment and made sure he went to bed. Well Jessie Ann, although not extremely verbal, was obviously unhappy at the decision and felt that the center should be a little more lenient with clients who were drunk and disorderly and let them sleep at the center. Mitch told her that this was not the procedure. This was not detox. If she wanted to change that, she should speak to the administration.

The next day, the administration actually spoke to Mitch about this incident and made it sound again as if he was being too rough on the clients. It must be said at this point that Mitch's tolerance with the whole situation was becoming quite strained. Mitch had crossed the line himself several years ago, almost a dozen years ago to be exact, when his wife and he were separated, and he had an affair with someone at another organization. This was brought back in Technicolor by Jessie Ann and her boss, Tammi Jean, in retribution for Mitch's perceived insubordinate attitude toward Jessie Ann. They felt it necessary to tell Mitch's boss about it and embellished it to the ninth degree. The facts they presented were so skewed and biased as to be ridiculous. Thankfully, although it was mentioned to Mitch (by the administration), the incident was not taken seriously. Yet it began an already increasing dislike for the job and his situation. If these were the type of people who would try to get revenge for a slight Mitch himself didn't even know he had committed, imagine what else they were capable of.

Mitch sometimes felt like he was beset on all sides: from the top with the administration, from below with clients, and sideways from the staff and disharmony in the union with the steward, Mary, who was out to get him rather than help him. Mitch had always had a touch of hypertension and a bit of an anxiety issue, but with the constant barrage of problems that were not now part of being a frontline worker, he found his tolerance growing extremely thin. Trina was not the help that Julie used to be. In fact, when there was trouble, she would more often than not hide up in her office, as in the case of Scottie Mactavish.

Scottie was a schizophrenic who needed to be on his meds in order to act somewhat normally. He walked around in a tattered old kilt, had unruly, long, bright red hair, and seldom bathed. One night, when he came to book in, not only was he not on his meds, he was stoned and drunk. Mitch made the decision to book him in but with a warning, "Scottie, you go directly to bed and stay out of trouble and you will be allowed in for the night." Instead, he went up to use the phone outside the caseworker's office. Scottie began banging on the door of the caseworker's office as if he would break it down at any moment. Trina was calling the front desk frantically and Mitch told her the police were on the way and he would be up there in a short time. Mitch called Richard, one of the guards from the third floor. Trina had locked the caseworker's office but by time Mitch and Richard got there, Scottie had almost broken the glass. An argument began again with whoever he was talking with on the phone. It became a full-scale battle. He was asking his father if he could stay for another night at his place and he was refused. Scottie went crazy and smashed the phone down, breaking the receiver. In the meantime, the police came. Scottie left to building crying and screaming but went with the police. His father showed up after the fact.

Before Mitch's next shift, some news reached the center. Luis Escobar had died days after the incident at the center. Cause of death was listed as accidental by the housing and city people. The true cause of death was overdose from booze and pills. The next person Mitch had to deal with was a Cuban fellow named Gabriel Rivera who thought that he was Tony Montana from the "Scarface" movie. He was in the house for several days and was allowed to do pretty well as he pleased. He was drunk and disorderly, constantly threatening other clients and always late for curfew. He would do his laundry in the middle of the night, waking everyone up, and he was generally belligerent and confrontational.

One night, when Mitch was on shift and was locking up at 11:00 p.m., Gabriel was drunk and sleeping on a washing machine. Mitch had about enough of Gabriel by this time and asked him to leave the facility. Mitch could not bar him for any more than twenty-four hours without management approval. He made a suggestion of one week, however, in his incident report. As Mitch was escorting Gabriel to the door, the verbal abuse that Mitch had to take was even more than usual. He was called everything from a goof to a queer and a lot of other things. The final straw only made Mitch laugh, however. As if Tony Montana himself had stepped out of Scarface, Gabriel said, "I am Cuban and I can do whatever I want. You a piece of chit," he said in his Cuban accent. Mitch began laughing and his laughing became hysterical and then maniacal. Mitch was cracking; there was no doubt about it. This only infuriated Gabriel further but he left without incident, cursing and verbally abusing all the way out the door.

Harry was an older employee with whom Mitch had a good relationship. He worked on the community soup van and homeless folks waited at certain checkpoints while he drove around with a small group of volunteers and fed them during the evenings. Harry was a retired fireman and a nice old fellow who brought his wife on his runs with the soup van. He was paid, though not much, but he wanted to help. They had a lot of fun, Mitch and Harry.

When Mitch appealed to the administration to have Fridays off because of his need to help his family—his mother and his mother-in-law were ill and his wife was not well—Harry's response would be something like, "Long weekend again, eh." When Mitch did show up the odd Friday, Harry would say, "I must be hallucinating. Is this really Friday?" It was all in good fun. Harry didn't know Mitch's circumstances and Mitch got a kick out of Harry.

One night, a particularly drunk client who was not presently staying at the center asked for food after Harry had already pulled the van into the center for the evening. Harry had no food left. When he gave this response to the client, the client became belligerent and abusive and called Harry's wife a liar. He then placed himself in front of the van so that Harry could not properly park it in the parking spot. When Harry tried to move the van, he inched ahead slowly so the client wouldn't be hurt. As soon as the van had moved an inch, the client made a huge show of pretending that he was hit by the van and fell down feigning serious injury. He was not injured, of course. The police were called and this being a Friday night when Mitch liked to get out at 11:00 p.m., it meant that he had to stay and do reports on the incident and speak to the police. He ended up staying until 12:30 p.m. Trina left at 11:00 as usual, waving goodbye as she drove away. The police did not take the client seriously. He was obviously not injured. Harry and Mitch both shook their heads at the things they had to put up with to try to help without any support or understanding from Administration. They should have to do some of these shifts.

Sometimes, Mitch's faith in God was the only thing that saved him from going completely mad. Jeannie, Mitch's wife, was a woman of God also, and a rock who was always there and supported him. Mitch always thought that the Lord was saving him for something, but he was not sure what it was yet. He knew somehow, though, that he had to get through these trials to get there. Calls from Julie, Lou Ann, and Nick also helped immensely. Trina had now gone full time with the city and was an off-site housing caseworker. Mitch's temporary replacement was Priscilla. Things only got worse after that until the point Mitch felt that his health was worsening. The doctor had informed Mitch that his hypertension had reached epic proportions and that his anxiety was not helping, especially with such a stressful job. This was the situation Mitch was in as he moved into the last phase of his tenure at Redemption Center and the end of the Redemption Center as people on the outside would know it forever.

PART IV:
The Guardian Angel Level

Chapter One

So after a few months with no program director, the administration made a controversial decision. They were going with a shelter manager instead of a program director. The title would still be program director except the person would be more hands-on and hopefully from the ranks of those who had done the job. Interviews were held and Mitch put his hat in the ring, even though he was the union rep, just to see what the job would consist of. He had no intention of taking it. The interview by Mr. Bain, Mr. Watson, and the administrative assistant consisted mostly of scenario questions and how a manager would handle certain situations, especially of a confrontational nature. Mitch felt he did fairly well in the interview, yet he made it clear at the end of the interview that he had no interest in the job itself but had come to the interview to see what the job entailed. Whether he would have ever been considered seriously, considering his union affiliation, was something he would never know. The person who was most seriously considered was Rick. Rick was quite popular with the staff, and the administration felt that he was the right choice as a liaison between staff and administration.

Rick seemed to change the moment he got the job. He was not the person he used to be. His conversations with Mitch were now very business-like in nature—very generic. No feelings or true observations of the job, the clients, or the staff were shared between them. One night, Mitch felt it necessary to phone Rick from his afternoon shift on the desk. He phoned him at home and left a message and waited for reply. Rick did phone back later in the evening. Mitch stated his feelings. "Rick, it seems like you changed since you became program director. We don't talk anymore. Have I done something to offend you?" Rick's answer was, "Of course not." Mitch then realized that Rick was under a lot of pressure with his illness and that the Redemption Center was using him.

One day, when Mr. Watson was on the desk with Rick and Mitch came in for his afternoon shift just before the dinner line, Mr. Watson repeated almost verbatim an earlier speech. Mitch got a true picture of what was actually going on. Mr. Watson said, "You know, Mitch, this three days a week of yours is really hurting us. We're having a hard time finding people to replace your shifts, you're making things difficult for us."

Mitch's reply was, "I can't help it that I am ill. For you to bring that up again at a time like this only proves that you have no regard for my situation or the medical issues I might be going through.

I think this conversation is best ended now." Rick, who was always a vocal proponent of the underprivileged and the working man at large, stayed silent, though Mitch knew he agreed. Rick's comment to Mitch later was, "Make sure you have all your medical documentation in order. Then there is nothing they can do to you because but they're not happy about this development."

This conversation really shocked Mitch to his boots so that he didn't know what to say anymore. It seemed that there was no one left to count on except for his wife and a few good friends. He was alone at the Redemption Center. Priscilla, as previously mentioned, a middle-aged, well meaning, empathetic to the ninth degree worker made life more difficult for Mitch. One night when Priscilla could not work, Mitch really realized what she had done as far as spoiling and enabling the clients. It seemed that when she served snacks, she brought things from home as well as what was in the center. She made presentations with fancy dishes with fancy foil designs underneath them and trays with fancy desserts as well as pizza and all kinds of things clients didn't usually get. Not that this was wrong—it was very magnanimous of her. However, it set the bar too high and other staff had a hard time living up to it, besides the fact the clients now expected this all the time and between the funding and the availability, it was simply not possible. One night, when Priscilla was off sick, Mitch found himself in a dual situation.

There was no case manager and Mario, a trainee, had never served snack, so Mitch had to do it this rare time. He took what was available in the kitchen, like some pastries and some leftover pizza, and served it. The comments from the clients were: this is not a very good presentation, this is not near what Priscilla would serve. Mitch's comment was, "This is not a five-star restaurant and I'm not a chef. So be thankful for what you have because I would certainly eat it and many others certainly would also."

At the next union-management meeting, Mr. Watson made a great show of announcing how the city was going to change the center and we had better be ready. All clients had to be accepted, no matter what the circumstance. Mr. Bain was at this meeting also and reiterated how in the past, the city had simply allocated funds for the Redemption Center to run homeless housing within the shelter but now this was all about to change. Mr. Bain's perception of this was that it was not good and that the administration was fearful of it because it would compromise their Christian beliefs and the way they ran the center with a Christian focus. Mr. Watson's opinion was that what the city was asking them to do was not unreasonable, another example of his administrative naiveté.

All the other shelters had been prepared for this for a long time and had developed their own rules to continue to keep order within the shelter and still seemed like they were complying with the city. But Mr. Watson, afraid of the ramifications of not totally playing ball with the city, had sold out. He was willing to do whatever they asked him and as a result, the other shelters took full advantage of his lack of knowledge and dumped clients on the Redemption Center like never before. Drunken clients,

clients with mental health issues and addictions, violent clients, and those who had been barred from every other facility were totally accepted at Redemption Center. Further, the drop-in center, which was the Beasly Center, traditionally kept these types of clients on mats overnight with plenty of staff and police right down the street. It was now closing. They couldn't handle the neighborhood complaints or the violence and disorder that their shelter was forced to deal with. They were closing the overnight portion of the shelter and it would remain a day drop-in only. This meant that all the clients that were basically street people and not fit for any other shelter because of their behavior, now came to the Redemption Center.

The Jesus Saves Kitchen and the New Apostles Center had prepared for this. Jesus Saves Kitchen had a drug and alcohol program and only thirty beds. The New Apostles Center had only forty beds. Both shelters made sure that they handpicked their clients early in the evening, also. So Redemption Center, with its 120 beds became the dupe. The staff all knew it; just the administration was in denial.

The city folks, led by Tammi Jean, were now in control and it was either accept their verdict or be shut down, as one of the shelters was predicted to be. Mr. Watson and Mr. Bain feared that it would be the Redemption Center. Mitch lost a lot of respect for the Redemption Center at that point because he had always considered them a Christian organization, however confused, and that in the end, they would stand for the precepts they preached and the mission statement that they seemed to believe. Yet when the time came, they seemed to sell out without even a fight. By doing this, they placed their staff in an extremely precarious situation. If it was bad before, it was worse than ever now. The thing that Mitch really didn't understand was how an iconic organization like this in the community, and even in the world at large, could be bullied into this kind of behavior simply to keep the money train continuing. Mitch had to admit also that he was disappointed in Rick having considered him a friend and also a friend to the people or the working man, a union man. How could someone change like that so drastically? If the

Redemption Center had decided to fight the new edicts that had come down from the city, the front page news would have been devastating to the city: "City closes Redemption Center because it would not cooperate or compromise its Christian values and the way they deal with clients and staff at their center." Instead, they chose not to fight and Mitch felt it acutely and there was no one to really go to.

When Mitch saw what his co-workers and the clients were going through, and Nick Smith at the Jesus Saves Kitchen, he was beside himself with the lack of justice within the system. So that he understood that this was simply not a client issue, the clients agreed with him, also. Most would have thought that this situation needed to be taken under control. Mitch's tolerance and ability a deal with the situation became more frayed day by day, until it reached a head and he could deal with it no more.

Chapter Two

Rick didn't realize it but the administration was using him. Every dirty job the administration had to do, from disciplining clients to disciplining staff, to dealing with emergency situations and being called in overnight, was relegated to Rick. He was not a program director as they made him think. He was the front man so that Mr. Watson and Mr. Bain didn't have to deal with the really messy business of homelessness. Rick must have realized at this point, though he did not admit it. Mitch, who sincerely liked Rick, only became confused by the situation. Rick seemed to cut off all communication with everyone outside of his own circle because the staff and the administration had turned on him. He was still a union man at heart, and it was hard for him to swallow the hypocrisy to believe considering the stance that he now took on issues. Rick supposedly had an incurable disease, a rare type of cancer. He had a good pension from the factory and was retired and there was really no reason for him to do this. He was bored and had nothing else to do, but he didn't sign up for this abuse. Mitch had to believe that all this was hurting Rick, and his change in attitude at meetings and his severing of relationships proved this.

What was happening at the Redemption Center upset Mitch a lot. If there was one place Mitch always believed would hold fast to its original mandate and mission statement, it was the Redemption Center. Many people were not aware of this, but Mitch and his wife, as young folks during the hippie era, had been married at Redemption Center. No one else would marry them at that time during the early seventies—1972 to be exact. No one would marry them because they were young—Mitch was twenty and Jeannie was only nineteen—until an officer at the Redemption Center did marry them. Other than the Jesus

Saves Kitchen and even beyond the respect he had for them in the beginning, Mitch respected the Redemption Center more. In the past, they had always stood for justice and helping the poor and not just the poor, but those who had fallen through the cracks and needed help in mainstream society. They had always preached a Christian message and tried to live by a Christian integrity. It seemed that all that had changed recently. They had become just like everyone else. Christianity was not even spoken of in their daily business and their alliance with the city and their willingness to do what the city suggested at any cost seemed hypocritical. In the end, Mitch thought that they had sold out, just like everyone else. It was a sad reality that it took a long time for Mitch to accept.

Mr. Watson made Mitch's three days a week as difficult as he could because he didn't want Mitch to have a three-day workweek, no matter what his medical situation was. Instead of letting him work Monday, Tuesday, and Wednesday, which would have left the latter part of the week for taking care of his medical appointments and taking care of his mom and his wife, Mr. Watson gave him Mondays, Wednesdays, and Fridays as his part-time hours. Fridays were the most difficult shift of the week. Clients often returned drunk and disorderly. It was never clear whether Mr. Watson, Mr. Bain, and even Rick took Mitch's situation seriously and believed that he really had a medical situation, even though he had all of the doctor's documentation. One of Mr. Watson's last and most hurtful comments was that Mitch was not really a union employee but simply a volunteer and he did it because he wanted to and if he didn't like it and it was causing him stress, he should resign. He took no complicity for what was happening at the center or why so many staff had quit or been disgruntled at the situations that took place.

The Redemption Center administration and the officers who worked for them totally stonewalled and stayed in denial of any complicity of anything that went wrong at the center and when they were proved wrong, they never admitted it anyway. They put the staff out there on the frontline in the most difficult set of conditions and then when things didn't go the way they should, it was always the staff that was to blame. There was never any complicity by the organization. To the Redemption Center, the clients were the cash cow and staff had very little value and could be disposed of very quickly.

One of the last shifts that Mitch ever worked on the desk, he was with Trina, who was doing an odd shift just before she went to the city as an off-site housing worker. Police had been called to remove Richard Arliss, one of Debbie's favorites, who was drunk and disorderly again and disrupting the whole hostel in the middle of the night by starting a party in the dorm that his room was adjacent to. Trina called Mitch from the caseworker's office to eject him from the facility, but he would not leave without his belongings and there was a ton of them. When the police showed up saying that they would not arrest him but take him to another facility, Trina asked Mitch to go up and get his belongings. Mitch was not feeling well as it was, with his hypertension reaching epic proportions. Although he didn't know it then, his anxiety was aggravating his blood pressure. Still, Mitch went up and packed the belongings while the police waited. There were several garbage bags and several suitcases plus a locker full of miscellaneous bike tools, equipment, hygienic supplies, and other belongings, including a bottle of booze and a crack pipe. Still, Mitch did what he was told and packed the equipment. Mitch delivered them to the curb where Richard was waiting with the police. Mitch was exhausted. He got a "fuck you, Mitch" from Richard for his efforts and a noncommittal response from police. Richard was taken away but Mitch was at the end of his tether that night. He was out of breath and felt he was going to faint. He didn't know if it was a panic attack or a frustration attack.

Trina was down at the front desk to keep control of it while Mitch was dealing with all this. It seemed like no sooner was Richard gone then another two clients showed up at the front desk for admittance to the center. Police were still out front dealing with Richard and his belongings when they showed up. Justin and Randy were their names. They didn't appear too inebriated, at least Randy didn't, so Mitch allowed Randy in, even though he was drunk and stoned, and he was allowed to go to bed and that's just what he did—he went directly to bed.

Justin was another story. This was not the first time that Justin had done this. He knew better and Mitch intended to call him on it because his influence was enabling other clients to do the same thing. If Mitch didn't make an issue this time, it would be impossible to keep order. Trina, who was standing beside Mitch, caught the whole conversation, but Justin was her client and she tended to have a soft spot for him.

Mitch refused him entrance based on the state that he was in. Justin's response was, "You think you're tough because the cops are outside. I will get you later." Trina's response was, "Don't take this seriously. It's just the way that Justin challenges." Without the support of the caseworker, Mitch's response was to allow him in as long as he went directly to bed. However, Mitch had a reaction to the situation and it wasn't fear because he wasn't afraid of Justin. He had dealt with these types of situations many times before. It was an accumulation of the amount of abuse and traumatic things that Mitch had seen during his tenure as a worker. He had a panic attack of sorts and couldn't breathe. His co-worker, Trina, thought he might be having a heart attack and her response was, "I hope you're not having a heart attack." Not that she cared about Mitch, but that would mean that she would have to handle the shift alone and do all the reports and take care of Mitch and call him an ambulance, which she wouldn't want to do.

It wasn't so much what had happened but the accumulation of things and the feeling of helplessness, that the worker had no authority or power whatsoever and the client could do whatever he wanted including death threats, however veiled. Mitch's breakdown was based on that. The structure that he had once known in this business was now finished and he had been doing this for eighteen years. Was he helping anyone and was anything really being accomplished for the client or the staff? He left work that night feeling very ill and went to the doctor the next day. His hypertension had reached epic proportions and finally, after five different kinds of meds prescribed for him, they still could not get his hypertension or high blood pressure down. As a result, he was at risk of heart attack and stroke, also. Mitch was ordered to go off work permanently, until further notice. He phoned the administration at that time (the executive assistant secretary to be exact) and told her exactly what was going on. The only response from Mr. Watson was, "Make sure your doctor's reports are submitted on time." Mr. Watson remained uncommitted and unsympathetic. After that point, Mitch never heard from Mr. Watson or Mr. Bain ever again. In the eight months that he was absent, he had to undergo treatment and counseling for his hypertension and anxiety disorder and was basically diagnosed with post traumatic stress disorder. There was not even a phone call from the Redemption Center. The point was that their insurance premiums went up and they were upset with Mitch. In the eight months that Mitch was off following this incident, an understanding and reconciliation within himself and an enlightenment of sorts came upon him in regard to his whole eighteen years in the helping professions, not just at the Redemption Center but at all the agencies he had worked at. He spent a lot of time in prayer and meditation and let the Spirit of God heal him. What being a helper was intended to be and what it became was not up to him, nor could he control it. What he gleaned from it, however, was his own spiritual evolution and growth, in other words, spiritual maturity.

Chapter Three: Reprise

So what had Mitch learned in his many years in the system? He had lasted longer than most anyone he knew. Had he helped mankind? To a large degree, he believed he had. Could he change the system, however? No, he could not. Still his contribution was not forgotten because many an employee called him after the fact to see how he was and to tell him the state of things, which had disintegrated to the point where it was almost unfathomable to work at the Redemption Center anymore. Some of the clients he ran into missed him, also.

Some of Mitch's predictions had come true, also. There was now a 24-hour security guard on duty at the front door and many a staff had been verbally abused or physically attacked in his absence. Rick also, when he was finally convinced of the hypocrisy of the Redemption Center, quit on the spot. Then Mitch realized the true purpose of his tenure in the social work world—it was to tell others about the unsung heroes who were never spoken of and to educate new workers coming in and the public at large about the reality of social work.

It was always the great things the agencies had done for the poor that the public heard about. They were promoting their name and, of course, the plight of the client. Mitch intended to tell the story of the worker and the client. It was the just and honest thing to do, as far as Mitch was concerned. After many months of purging himself from his experiences through meditation and Christian prayer, Mitch also gained perspective on the true nature of helping. Helping was not just for the clients but for the worker, also, and that is what administrations did not understand. There were many more lucrative work situations to work at than those that went into social work.

These people wanted to help and the evolution of the worker on a spiritual/mental level was as important as the helping of the client. For this, an honest Christian leadership was necessary and unfortunately, many of the Christian organizations, not just shelters but churches and other Christian organizations, had become corrupt and had forgotten their first place or their original mandate: to feed a client not just with food but with the Christian spiritual message; to reinvest the client in honest dignity so that the client would be empowered to be a better person, and a worker would be proud of the job they did.

It was obvious that the system was not easy to change and there were too many people within it who were only there to climb the social ladder. If you could not change the system, you could still help an individual or many individuals, one by one. And that was the truth of the matter. In the end, if you could help put one on the road to their own dignity and self worth and belief in a spiritual renewal and redemption, you would have accomplished your mission.

Mitch, at fifty-seven years old, finally realized who and what he was. He was a helper who had put his heart on the line to see others fulfilled. He had helped many but even if it had only been one, it would have been worth the effort. The helping professions are not for fame or riches or even the acceptance of your peers. In recalling the story and realizing what he had learned, he realized that this knowledge was the purpose or end result of what he had been through. He didn't know all this then. He was too busy fighting for causes, but the Scripture that rang true now was, 1 Cor. 13:11. "When I was a child, I spake as a child, I understood as a child, I thought as a child: but when I was a man, I put away childish things."

This is the hope and it goes with true hearts. The Spirit of God can still change the world, even if it is only one person at a time, or a dozen, or thousands, through us. It is not for sale or gain or recognition. It is unconditional and without agenda. Because when the love of God has branded the heart within you who are his temple to share that love freely with others, then you have reached The Guardian Angel Level.

CPSIA information can be obtained at www.ICGtesting.com
Printed in the USA
LVOW040012021111

253064LV00002B/15/P